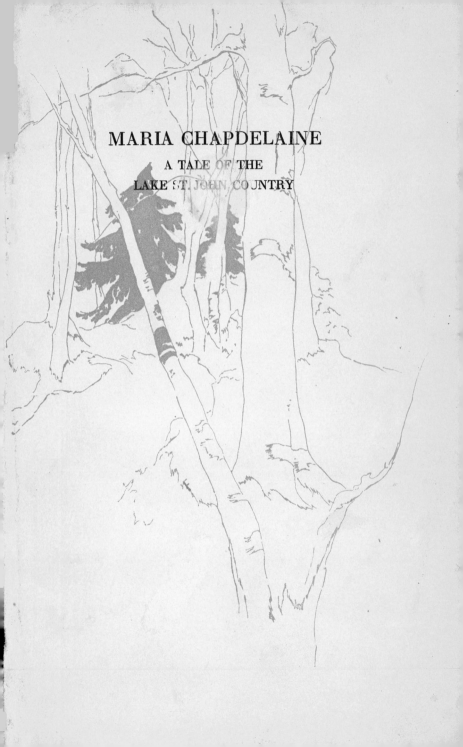

MARIA CHAPDELAINE

A TALE OF THE
LAKE ST. JOHN COUNTRY

THE MACMILLAN COMPANY
NEW YORK · BOSTON · CHICAGO · DALLAS
ATLANTA · SAN FRANCISCO

MACMILLAN & CO., LIMITED
LONDON · BOMBAY · CALCUTTA
MELBOURNE

THE MACMILLAN CO. OF CANADA, LTD.
TORONTO

MARIA CHAPDELAINE

A TALE OF THE
LAKE ST. JOHN COUNTRY

BY

LOUIS HÉMON

TRANSLATED BY
W. H. BLAKE

DRAWINGS BY
WILFRED JONES

New York
THE MACMILLAN COMPANY
1924

15266

CONTENTS

CHAPTER I
PERIBONKA

CHAPTER I

PERIBONKA

Ite, missa est

THE door opened, and the men of the congregation began to come out of the church at Peribonka. A moment earlier it had seemed quite deserted, this church set by the roadside on the high bank of the Peribonka, whose icy snow-covered surface was like a winding strip of plain. The snow lay deep upon road and fields, for the April sun was powerless to send warmth through the gray clouds, and the heavy spring rains were yet to come. This chill and universal white, the humbleness of the wooden church and the wooden houses scattered along the road, the gloomy forest edging so close that it seemed to threaten, these all spoke of a harsh existence in a stern land. But as the men and boys passed through the doorway and gathered in knots on the broad steps, their cheery salutations, the chaff flung from group to group, the continual in-

[3]

terchange of talk, merry or sober, at once
disclosed the unquenchable joyousness of a
people ever filled with laughter and good
humour.

Cleophas Pesant, son of Thadée Pesant
the blacksmith, was already in light-coloured
summer garments, and sported an American
coat with broad padded shoulders; though on
this cold Sunday he had not ventured to dis-
card his winter cap of black cloth with hare-
lined ear-laps for the hard felt hat he would
have preferred to wear. Beside him Egide
Simard, and others who had come a long
road by sleigh, fastened their long fur coats
as they left the church, drawing them in at
the waist with scarlet sashes. The young
folk of the village, very smart in coats with
otter collars, gave deferential greeting to old
Nazaire Larouche; a tall man with gray hair
and huge bony shoulders who had in no wise
altered for the mass his everyday garb: short
jacket of brown cloth lined with sheepskin,
patched trousers, and thick woollen socks
under moose-hide moccasins.

"Well, Mr. Larouche, do things go pretty
well across the water?"

[4]

"Not badly, my lads, not so badly."

Everyone drew his pipe from his pocket, and the pig's bladder filled with tobacco leaves cut by hand, and, after the hour and a half of restraint, began to smoke with evident satisfaction. The first puffs brought talk of the weather, the coming spring, the state of the ice on Lake St. John and the rivers, of their several doings and the parish gossip; after the manner of men who, living far apart on the worst of roads, see one another but once a week.

"The lake is solid yet," said Cleophas Pesant, "but the rivers are no longer safe. The ice went this week beside the sand-bank opposite the island, where there have been warm spring-holes all winter." Others began to discuss the chances of the crops, before the ground was even showing.

"I tell you that we shall have a lean year," asserted one old fellow, "the frost got in before the last snows fell."

At length the talk slackened and all faced the top step, where Napoleon Laliberté was making ready, in accord with his weekly custom, to announce the parish news. He stood there motionless for a little while, awaiting quiet,—hands deep in the pockets of the heavy lynx coat, knitting his forehead and half closing his keen eyes under the fur cap pulled well over his ears; and when silence fell he began to give the news at the full pitch of his voice, in the manner of a carter who encourages his horses on a hill.

"The work on the wharf will go forward at once . . . I have been sent money by the Government, and those looking for a job should see me before vespers. If you want this money to stay in the parish instead of being sent back to Quebec you had better lose no time in speaking to me."

Some moved over in his direction; others, indifferent, met his announcement with a laugh. The remark was heard in an envious undertone:—"And who will be foreman at three dollars a day? Perhaps good old Laliberté . . ."

But it was said jestingly rather than in malice, and the speaker ended by adding his own laugh.

Hands still in the pockets of his big coat, straightening himself and squaring his shoulders as he stood there upon the highest step, Napoleon Laliberté proceeded in loudest tones:—"A surveyor from Roberval will be in the parish next week. If anyone wishes his land surveyed before mending his fences for the summer, this is to let him know."

The item was received without interest. Peribonka farmers are not particular about correcting their boundaries to gain or lose a few square feet, since the most enterprising among them have still two-thirds of their grants to clear,—endless acres of woodland and swamp to reclaim.

He continued:—"Two men are up here with money to buy furs. If you have any bear, mink, muskrat or fox you will find these men at the store until Wednesday, or you can apply to François Paradis of Mistassini who is with them. They have plenty of money and will pay cash for first-class pelts." His news finished, he descended the steps. A sharp-faced little fellow took his place.

"Who wants to buy a fine young pig of my breeding?" he asked, indicating with his finger something shapeless that struggled in a bag at his feet. A great burst of laughter

[7]

greeted him. They knew them well, these pigs of Hormidas' raising. No bigger than rats, and quick as squirrels to jump the fences.

"Twenty-five cents!" one young man bid chaffingly.

"Fifty cents!"

"A dollar!"

"Don't play the fool, Jean. Your wife will never let you pay a dollar for such a pig as that."

Jean stood his ground:—"A dollar, I won't go back on it."

Hormidas Bérubé with a disgusted look on his face awaited another bid, but only got jokes and laughter.

Meantime the women in their turn had begun to leave the church. Young or old, pretty or ugly, nearly all were well clad in fur cloaks, or in coats of heavy cloth; for, honouring the Sunday mass, sole festival of their lives, they had doffed coarse blouses and homespun petticoats, and a stranger might well have stood amazed to find them habited almost with elegance in this remote spot; still French to their finger-tips in the midst of the vast

lonely forest and the snow, and as taste-
fully dressed, these peasant women, as
most of the middle-class folk in provincial
France.

Cleophas Pesant waited for Louisa Tremblay who was alone, and they went off together along the wooden sidewalk in the direction of the house. Others were satisfied
to exchange jocular remarks with the young
girls as they passed, in the easy and familiar
fashion of the country,—natural enough too
where the children have grown up together
from infancy.

Pite Gaudreau, looking toward the door of
the church, remarked:—"Maria Chapdelaine
is back from her visit to St. Prime, and there is
her father come to fetch her." Many in the
village scarcely knew the Chapdelaines.

"Is it Samuel Chapdelaine who has a farm
in the woods on the other side of the river,
above Honfleur?"

"That's the man."

"And the girl with him is his daughter?
Maria . . ."

"Yes, she has been spending a month at St.
Prime with her mother's people. They are

Bouchards, related to Wilfrid Bouchard of
St. Gedeon . . ."

Interested glances were directed toward
the top of the steps. One of the young people
paid Maria the countryman's tribute of ad-
miration:—"A fine hearty girl!" said he.

"Right you are! A fine hearty girl, and
one with plenty of spirit too. A pity that she
lives so far off in the woods. How are the
young fellows of the village to manage an
evening at their place, on the other side of the
river and above the falls, more than a dozen
miles away and the last of them with next to
no road?"

The smiles were bold enough as they spoke
of her, this inaccessible beauty; but as she
came down the wooden steps with her father
and passed near by, they were taken with
bashfulness and awkwardly drew back, as
though something more lay between her and
them than the crossing of a river and twelve
miles of indifferent woodland road.

Little by little the groups before the church
dissolved. Some returned to their houses,
after picking up all the news that was going;
others, before departing, were for spending an

hour in one of the two gathering places of the village; the *curé's* house or the general store. Those who came from the back concessions, stretching along the very border of the forest, one by one untied their horses from the row and brought their sleighs to the foot of the steps for their women and children.

Samuel Chapdelaine and Maria had gone but a little way when a young man halted them.

"Good day to you, Mr. Chapdelaine. Good day, Miss Maria. I am in great luck at meeting you, since your farm is so high up the river and I don't often come this way myself."

His bold eyes travelled from one to the other. When he averted them it seemed by a conscious effort of politeness; swiftly they returned, and their glance, bright, keen, full of honest eagerness, was questioning and disconcerting.

"François Paradis!" exclaimed Chapdelaine.

"This is indeed a bit of luck, for I haven't seen you this long while, François. And your father dead too. Have you held on to the farm?"

The young man did not answer; he was looking expectantly at Maria with a frank smile, awaiting a word from her.

"You remember François Paradis of Mistassini, Maria? He has changed very little."

"Nor have you, Mr. Chapdelaine. But your daughter, that is a different story; she is not the same, yet I should have known her at once."

They had spent the last evening at St. Michel de Mistassini—viewing everything in the full light of the afternoon: the great wooden bridge, covered in and painted red, not unlike an amazingly long Noah's ark; the high hills rising almost from the very banks of the river, the old monastery crouched between the river and the heights, the water that seethed and whitened, flinging itself in wild descent down the staircase of a giant. But to see this young man after seven years, and to hear his name spoken, aroused in Maria memories clearer and more lively than she was able to evoke of the events and sights of yesterday.

"François Paradis! . . . Why surely, father, I remember François Paradis." And

François, content, gave answer to the questions of a moment ago.

"No, Mr. Chapdelaine, I have not kept the farm. When the good man died I sold everything, and since then I have been nearly all the time in the woods, trapping or bartering with the Indians of Lake Mistassini and the Rivière aux Foins. I also spent a couple of years in the Labrador." His look passed once more from Samuel Chapdelaine to Maria, and her eyes fell.

"Are you going home to-day?" he asked.

"Yes; right after dinner."

"I am glad that I saw you, for I shall be passing up the river near your place in two or three weeks, when the ice goes out. I am here with some Belgians who are going to buy furs from the Indians; we shall push up so soon as the river is clear, and if we pitch a tent above the falls close to your farm I will spend the evening with you."

"That is good, François, we will expect you."

The alders formed a thick and unbroken hedge along the river Peribonka; but the leafless stems did not shut away the steeply sloping bank, the levels of the frozen river, the dark hem of the woods crowding to the farther edge—leaving between the solitude of the great trees, thick-set and erect, and the bare desolateness of the ice only room for a few narrow fields, still for the most part uncouth with stumps, so narrow indeed that they seemed to be constrained in the grasp of an unkindly land.

To Maria Chapdelaine, glancing inattentively here and there, there was nothing in all this to make one feel lonely or afraid. Never had she known other prospect from October to May, save those still more depressing and sad, farther yet from the dwellings of man and the marks of his labour; and moreover all about her that morning had taken on a softer outline, was brighter with a new promise, by virtue of something sweet and gracious that the future had in its keeping. Perhaps the coming springtime . . . perhaps another happiness that was stealing toward her, nameless and unrecognized.

Samuel Chapdelaine and Maria were to dine with their relative Azalma Larouche, at whose house they had spent the night. No one was there but the hostess, for many years a widow, and old Nazaire Larouche, her brother-in-law. Azalma was a tall, flat-chested woman with the undeveloped features of a child, who talked very quickly and almost without taking breath while she made ready the meal in the kitchen. From time to time she halted her preparations and sat down opposite her visitors, less for the moment's repose than to give some special emphasis to what she was about to say; but the seasoning of a dish or the setting of the table speedily claimed her attention again, and the monologue went on amid the clatter of dishes and frying-pans.

The pea-soup was soon ready and on the table. While eating, the two men talked about the condition of their farms and the state of the spring ice.

"You should be safe enough for crossing this evening," said Nazaire Larouche, "but it will be touch-and-go, and I think you will be about the last. The current is strong below the fall and already we have had three days of rain."

[15]

"Everybody says that the ice will hold for a long time yet," replied his sister-in-law. "Better sleep here again to-night, and after supper the young folks from the village will drop in and spend the evening. It is only fair that Maria should have a little more amusement before you drag her off into your woods up there."

"She has had plenty of gaiety at St. Prime; singing and games almost every night. We are greatly obliged to you, but I am going to put the horse in immediately after dinner so as to get home in good time."

Old Nazaire Larouche spoke of the morning's sermon which had struck him as well reasoned and fine; then after a spell of silence he exclaimed abruptly:—"Have you baked?"

His amazed sister-in-law gaped at him for a moment before it stole upon her that this was his way of asking for bread. A little later he attacked her with another question:—"Is your pump working well?"

Which signified that there was no water on the table. Azalma rose to get it, and behind her back the old fellow sent a sly wink in the

[16]

direction of Maria. "I assault her with par-
ables," chuckled he. "It's politer."

On the plank walls of the house were pasted
old newspapers, and calendars hung there
such as the manufacturers of farm implements
or grain merchants scatter abroad, and also
prints of a religious character; a representation in crudest colour and almost innocent of
perspective of the basilica at Ste. Anne de
Beaupré; a likeness of Pope Pius X.; a chromo
where the palely-smiling Virgin Mary disclosed her bleeding heart encircled with a
golden nimbus.

"This is nicer than our house," thought
Maria to herself.

Nazaire Larouche kept directing attention
to his wants with dark sayings:—"Was your
pig very lean?" he demanded; or perhaps:—
"Fond of maple sugar, are you? I never get
enough of it . . ."

And then Azalma would help him to a second slice of pork or fetch the cake of maple
sugar from the cupboard. When she wearied
of these strange table-manners and bade him
help himself in the usual fashion, he smoothed
her ruffled temper with good-humoured excuses.

[17]

"Quite right. Quite right. I won't do it again; but you always loved a joke, Azalma. When you have youngsters like me at dinner you must look for a little nonsense."

Maria smiled to think how like he was to her father; both tall and broad, with grizzled hair, their faces tanned to the colour of leather, and, shining from their eyes, the quenchless spirit of youth which keeps alive in the countryman of Quebec his imperishable simple-heartedness.

They took the road almost as soon as the meal was over. The snow, thawed on top by the early rains, and frozen anew during the cold nights, gave an icy surface that slipped away easily beneath the runners. The high blue hills on the other side of Lake St. John which closed the horizon behind them were gradually lost to view as they returned up the long bend of the river.

Passing the church, Samuel Chapdelaine said thoughtfully:—"The mass is beautiful. I am often very sorry that we live so far from churches. Perhaps not being able to attend to our religion every Sunday hinders us from being just so fortunate as other people."

[18]

"It is not our fault," sighed Maria, "we are too far away."

Her father shook his head regretfully. The imposing ceremonial, the Latin chants, the lighted tapers, the solemnity of the Sunday mass never failed to fill him with exaltation. In a little he began to sing:—

> J'irai la voir un jour,
> M'asseoir près de son trône,
> Recevoir ma couronne
> Et régner à mon tour . . .

His voice was strong and true, and he used the full volume of it, singing with deep fervour; but ere long his eyes began to close and his chin to drop toward his breast. Driving always made him sleepy, and the horse, aware that the usual drowsiness had possession of his master, slackened his pace and at length fell to a walk.

"Get up there, Charles Eugene!"

He had suddenly waked and put his hand out for the whip. Charles Eugene resigned himself and began to trot again. Many generations ago a Chapdelaine cherished a long feud with a neighbour who bore these names, and had forthwith bestowed them upon an

old, tired, lame horse of his, that he might give
himself the pleasure every day when passing
the enemy's house of calling out very loudly:
—"Charles Eugene, ill-favoured beast that
you are! Wretched, badly brought up creature! Get along, Charles Eugene!" For a
whole century the quarrel was dead and
buried; but the Chapdelaines ever since had
named their successive horses Charles Eugene.

Once again the hymn rose in clear ringing
tones, intense with feeling:—

> Au ciel, au ciel, au ciel,
> J'irai la voir un jour . . .

And again sleep was master, the voice died
away, and Maria gathered up the reins
dropped from her father's hand.

The icy road held alongside the frozen river.
The houses on the other shore, each surrounded with its patch of cleared land, were
sadly distant from one another. Behind the
clearings, and on either side of them to the
river's bank, it was always forest: a dark
green background of cypress against which a
lonely birch tree stood out here and there, its
bole naked and white as the column of a
ruined temple.

On the other side of the road the strip of cleared land was continuous and broader; the houses, set closer together, seemed an outpost of the village; but ever behind the bare fields marched the forest, following like a shadow, a gloomy frieze without end between white ground and gray sky.

"Charles Eugene, get on there!"

Chapdelaine woke and made his usual good-humoured feint toward the whip; but by the time the horse slowed down, after a few livelier paces, he had dropped off again, his hands lying open upon his knees showing the worn palms of the horse-hide mittens, his chin resting upon the coat's thick fur.

After a couple of miles the road climbed a steep hill and entered the unbroken woods. The houses standing at intervals in the flat country all the way from the village came abruptly to an end, and there was no longer anything for the eye to rest upon but a wilderness of bare trunks rising out of the universal whiteness. Even the incessant dark green of balsam, spruce and gray pine was rare; the few young and living trees were lost among the endless dead, either lying on the ground

[21]

and buried in snow, or still erect but stripped
and blackened. Twenty years before great
forest fires had swept through, and the new
growth was only pushing its way amid the
standing skeletons and the charred down-
timber. Little hills followed one upon the
other, and the road was a succession of ups
and downs scarcely more considerable than
the slopes of an ocean swell, from trough to
crest, from crest to trough.

Maria Chapdelaine drew the cloak about
her, slipped her hands under the warm robe
of gray goat-skin and half closed her eyes.
There was nothing to look at; in the settlements new houses and barns might go up from
year to year, or be deserted and tumble into
ruin; but the life of the woods is so unhurried
that one must needs have more than the patience of a human being to await and mark its
advance.

Alone of the three travellers the horse
remained fully awake. The sleigh glided over
the hard snow, grazing the stumps on either
hand level with the track. Charles Eugene
accurately followed every turn of the road,
took the short pitches at a full trot and

climbed the opposite hills with a leisurely
pace, like the capable animal he was, who
might be trusted to conduct his masters safely
to the door-step of their dwelling without
being annoyed by guiding word or touch of
rein.

Some miles farther, and the woods fell
away again, disclosing the river. The road
descended the last hill from the higher land
and sank almost to the level of the ice. Three
houses were dotted along the mile of bank
above; but they were humbler buildings than
those of the village, and behind them scarcely
any land was cleared and there was little
sign of cultivation:—built there, they seemed
to be, only in witness of the presence of man.

Charles Eugene swung sharply to the right,
stiffened his forelegs to hold back on the slope
and pulled up on the edge of the ice. Chapdelaine opened his eyes.

"Here, father," said Maria, "take the
reins!" He seized them, but before giving his
horse the word, took some moments for a
careful scrutiny of the frozen surface.

"There is a little water on the ice," said he,
"and the snow has melted; but we ought to be

able to cross all the same. Get up, Charles
Eugene."

The horse lowered his head and sniffed at
the white expanse in front of him, then adven-
tured upon it without more ado. The ruts of
the winter road were gone, the little firs which
had marked it at intervals were nearly all
fallen and lying in the half-thawed snow; as
they passed the island the ice cracked twice
without breaking. Charles Eugene trotted
smartly toward the house of Charles Lindsay
on the other bank. But when the sleigh
reached midstream, below the great fall, the
horse had perforce to slacken pace by reason
of the water which had overflowed the ice and
wetted the snow. Very slowly they approached the shore; there remained only some
thirty feet to be crossed when the ice began
to go up and down under the horse's hoofs.

Old Chapdelaine, fully awake now, was on
his feet; his eyes beneath the fur cap shone
with courage and quick resolve.

"Go on, Charles Eugene! Go on there!" he
roared in his big voice. The wise beast dug his
calked shoes through the deep slush and
sprang for the bank, throwing himself into

the collar at every leap. Just as they reached
land a cake of ice tilted beneath their weight
and sank, leaving a space of open water.

Samuel Chapdelaine turned about. "We
are the last to cross this year," said he. And
he halted the horse to breathe before putting
him at the hill.

After following the main road a little way
they left it for another which plunged into the
woods. It was scarcely more than a rough
trail, still beset with roots, turning and twist-
ing in all directions to avoid boulders and
stumps. Rising to a plateau where it wound
back and forth through burnt lands it gave an
occasional glimpse of steep hillside, of the
rocks piled in the channel of the frozen rapid,
the higher and precipitous opposing slope
above the fall, and at the last resumed a
desolate way amid fallen trees and blackened
rampikes.

The little stony hillocks they passed
through seemed to close in behind them; the
burnt lands gave place to darkly-crowding
spruces and firs; now and then they caught
momentary sight of the distant mountains
on the Rivière Alec; and soon the travellers

discerned a clearing in the forest, a mounting column of smoke, the bark of a dog.

"They will be glad to see you again, Maria," said her father. "They have been lonesome for you, every one of them."

CHAPTER II
HOME IN THE CLEARING

CHAPTER II

HOME IN THE CLEARING

I T was supper-time before Maria had answered all the questions, told of her journey down to the last and littlest item, and given not only the news of St. Prime and Peribonka but everything else she had been able to gather up upon the road.

Tit'Bé, seated facing his sister, smoked pipe after pipe without taking his eyes off her for a single moment, fearful of missing some highly important disclosure that she had hitherto held back. Little Alma Rose stood with an arm about her neck; Telesphore was listening too, as he mended his dog's harness with bits of string. Madame Chapdelaine stirred the fire in the big cast-iron stove, came and went, brought from the cupboard plates and dishes, the loaf of bread and pitcher of milk, tilted the great molasses jar over a glass jug. Not seldom she stopped to ask Maria something, or to catch what she was saying, and stood for a few moments dreaming, hands on her hips, as the villages spoken of rose before her in memory.

". . . And so the church is finished—a beautiful stone church, with pictures on the walls and coloured glass in the windows . . . How splendid that must be! Johnny Bouchard built a new barn last year, and it is a little Perron, daughter of Abelard Perron of St. Jerome, who teaches school . . . Eight years since I was at St. Prime, just to think of it! A fine parish indeed, that would have suited me nicely; good level land as far as you can see, no rock cropping up and no bush, everywhere square-cornered fields with handsome straight fences and heavy soil. Only two hours' drive to the railway . . . Perhaps it is wicked of me to say so; but all my married life I have felt sorry that your father's taste was for moving, and pushing on and on into the woods, and not for living on a farm in one of the old parishes."

Through the little square window she threw a melancholy glance over the scanty cleared fields behind the house, the barn built of ill-joined planks that showed marks of fire, and the land beyond still covered with stumps and

[30]

encompassed by the forest, whence any return
of hay or grain could only be looked for at the
end of long and patient waiting.

"O look," said Alma Rose, "here is Chien
come for his share of petting." The dog laid
his long head with the sad eyes upon her knee;
uttering little friendly words, Maria bent and
caressed him.

"He has been lonely without you like the
rest of us," came from Alma Rose. "Every
morning he used to look at your bed to see
if you were not back." She called him to her.
"Come, Chien; come and let me pet you too."

Chien went obediently from one to the
other, half closing his eyes at each pat. Maria
looked about her to see if some change, un-
likely though that might be, had taken place
while she was away.

The great three-decked stove stood in the
centre of the house; the sheet-iron stove-pipe,
after mounting for some feet, turned at a
right angle and was carried through the house
to the outside, so that none of the precious
warmth should be lost. In a corner was the
large wooden cupboard; close by, the table; a
bench against the wall; on the other side of

the door the sink and the pump. A partition beginning at the opposite wall seemed designed to divide the house in two, but it stopped before reaching the stove and did not begin again beyond it, in such fashion that these divisions of the only room were each enclosed on three sides and looked like a stage setting—that conventional type of scene where the audience are invited to imagine that two distinct apartments exist although they look into both at once.

In one of these compartments the father and mother had their bed; Maria and Alma Rose in the other. A steep stairway ascended from a corner to the loft where the boys slept in the summer-time; with the coming of winter they moved their bed down and enjoyed the warmth of the stove with the rest of the family.

Hanging upon the wall were the illustrated calendars of shopkeepers in Roberval and Chicoutimi; a picture of the infant Jesus in his mother's arms—a rosy-faced Jesus with great blue eyes, holding out his chubby hands; a representation of some unidentified saint looking rapturously heavenward; the first page of

the Christmas number of a Quebec newspaper, filled with stars big as moons and angels
flying with folded wings.

"Were you a good girl while I was away,
Alma Rose?"

It was the mother who replied:—"Alma
Rose was not too naughty; but Telesphore
has been a perfect torment to me. It is not so
much that he does what is wrong; but the
things he says! One might suppose that the
boy had not all his wits."

Telesphore busied himself with the dog-
harness and made believe not to hear. Young
Telesphore's depravities supplied this household with its only domestic tragedy. To sat-
isfy her own mind and give him a proper con-
viction of besetting sin his mother had fash-
ioned for herself a most involved kind of
polytheism, had peopled the world with evil
spirits and good who influenced him alternately to err or to repent. The boy had come
to regard himself as a mere battleground
where devils who were very sly, and angels of
excellent purpose but little experience, waged
endless unequal warfare.

Gloomily would he mutter before the

empty preserve jar:—"It was the Demon of gluttony who tempted me."

Returning from some escapade with torn and muddy clothes he would anticipate reproach with his explanation:—"The Demon of disobedience lured me into that. Beyond doubt it was he." With the same breath asserting indignation at being so misled, and protesting the blamelessness of his intentions.

"But he must not be allowed to come back, eh, mother! He must not be allowed to come back, this bad spirit. I will take father's gun and I will shoot him . . ."

"You cannot shoot devils with a gun," objected his mother. "But when you feel the temptation coming, seize your rosary and say your prayers."

Telesphore did not dare to gainsay this; but he shook his head doubtfully. The gun seemed to him both the surer and the more amusing way, and he was accustomed to picture to himself a tremendous duel, a lingering slaughter from which he would emerge without spot or blemish, forever set free from the wiles of the Evil One.

Samuel Chapdelaine came into the house

and supper was served. The sign of the cross around the table; lips moving in a silent *Benedicite*, which Telesphore and Alma Rose repeated aloud; again the sign of the cross; the noise of chairs and bench drawn in; spoons clattering on plates. To Maria it was as though since her absence she was giving attention for the first time in her life to these sounds and movements; that they possessed a different significance from movements and sounds elsewhere, and invested with some peculiar quality of sweetness and peace all that happened in that house far off in the woods.

Supper was nearly at an end when a footstep sounded without; Chien pricked up his ears but gave no growl.

"A visitor," announced mother Chapdelaine, "Eutrope Gagnon has come over to see us."

It was an easy guess, as Eutrope Gagnon was their only neighbour. The year before he had taken up land two miles away, with his brother; the brother had gone to the shanties for the winter, and he was left alone in the cabin they had built of charred logs. He appeared on the threshold, lantern in hand.

"Greeting to each and all," was the salutation as he pulled off his woollen cap. "A fine night, and there is still a crust on the snow; as the walking was good I thought that I would drop in this evening to find out if you were back."

Although he came to see Maria, as all knew, it was to the father of the house that he directed his remarks, partly through shyness, partly out of deference to the manners of the country. He took the chair that was offered him.

"The weather is mild; if it misses turning wet it will be by very little. One can feel that the spring rains are not far off . . ."

It was the orthodox beginning to one of those talks among country folk which are like an interminable song, full of repetitions, each speaker agreeing with the words last uttered and adding more to the same effect. And naturally the theme was the Canadian's never-ending plaint; his protest, falling short of actual revolt, against the heavy burden of the long winter.

"The beasts have been in the stable since the end of October and the barn is just about

empty," said mother Chapdelaine. "Unless
spring comes soon I don't know what we are
going to do."

"Three weeks at least before they can be
turned out to pasture."

"A horse, three cows, a pig and the sheep,
without speaking of the fowls; it takes something to feed them!" this from Tit'Bé with
an air of grown-up wisdom.

He smoked and talked with the men now
by virtue of his fourteen years, his broad
shoulders and his knowledge of husbandry.
Eight years ago he had begun to care for the
stock, and to replenish the store of wood for
the house with the aid of his little sled.
Somewhat later he had learned to call *Heulle!
Heulle!* very loudly behind the thin-flanked
cows, and *Hue! Dia! Harrié!* when the horses
were ploughing; to manage a hay-fork and to
build a rail-fence. These two years he had
taken turn beside his father with ax and
scythe, driven the big wood-sleigh over the
hard snow, sown and reaped on his own
responsibility; and thus it was that no one
disputed his right freely to express an
opinion and to smoke incessantly the strong

leaf-tobacco. His face was still smooth as a child's, with immature features and guileless eyes, and one not knowing him would probably have been surprised to hear him speak with all the deliberation of an older and experienced man, and to see him ever-lastingly charging his wooden pipe; but in the Province of Quebec the boys are looked upon as men when they undertake men's work, and as to their precocity in smoking there is always the excellent excuse that it affords some protection in summer against the attacking swarms of black-flies, mos-quitos and sand-flies.

"How nice it would be to live in a country where there is hardly any winter, and where the earth makes provision for man and beast. Up here man himself, by dint of work, must care for his animals and his land. If we did not have Esdras and Da'Bé earning good wages in the woods how could we get along?"

"But the soil is rich in these parts," said Eutrope Gagnon.

"The soil is good but one must battle for it with the forest; and to live at all you must watch every copper, labour from morning to

night, and do everything yourself because
there is no one near to lend a hand."

Mother Chapdelaine ended with a sigh.
Her thoughts were ever fondly revisiting the
older parishes where the land has long been
cleared and cultivated, and where the houses
are neighbourly—her lost paradise.

Her husband clenched his fists and shook
his head with an obstinate gesture. "Only
you wait a few months . . . When the boys
are back from the woods we shall set to
work, they two, Tit'Bé and I, and presently
we shall have our land cleared. With four
good men ax in hand and not afraid of work
things will go quickly, even in the hard
timber. Two years from now there will be
grain harvested, and pasturage that will
support a good herd of cattle. I tell you
that we are going to make land."

"Make land!" Rude phrase of the country,
summing up in two words all the heart-
breaking labour that transforms the incult
woods, barren of sustenance, to smiling fields,
ploughed and sown. Samuel Chapdelaine's
eyes flamed with enthusiasm and determina-
tion as he spoke.

For this was the passion of his life; the passion of a man whose soul was in the clearing, not the tilling of the earth. Five times since boyhood had he taken up wild land, built a house, a stable and a barn, wrested from the unbroken forest a comfortable farm; and five times he had sold out to begin it all again farther north, suddenly losing interest; energy and ambition vanishing once the first rough work was done, when neighbours appeared and the countryside began to be opened up and inhabited. Some there were who entered into his feelings; others praised the courage but thought little of the wisdom, and such were fond of saying that if good sense had led him to stay in one place he and his would now be at their ease.

"At their ease . . ." O dread God of the Scriptures, worshipped by these countryfolk of Quebec without a quibble or a doubt, who hast condemned man to earn his bread in the sweat of his face, canst Thou for a moment smooth the awful frown from Thy forehead when Thou art told that certain of these Thy creatures have escaped the doom, and live at their ease?

"At their ease . . ." Truly to know what it means one must have toiled bitterly from dawn to dark with back and hands and feet, and the children of the soil are those who have best attained the knowledge. It means the burden lifted; the heavy burden of labour and of care. It means leave to rest, the which, even if it be unused, is a new mercy every moment. To the old it means so much of the pride of life as no one would deny them, the late revelation of unknown delights, an hour of idleness, a distant journey, a dainty or a purchase indulged in without anxious thought, the hundred and one things desirable that a competence assures.

So constituted is the heart of man that most of those who have paid the ransom and won liberty—ease—have in the winning of it created their own incapacity for enjoying the conquest, and toil on till death; it is the others, the ill-endowed or the unlucky, who have been unable to overcome fortune and escape their slavery, to whom the state of ease has all those charms of the inaccessible.

It may be that the Chapdelaines so were thinking, and each in his own fashion;

the father with the unconquerable optimism
of a man who knows himself strong and be-
lieves himself wise; the mother with a gentle
resignation; the others, the younger ones,
in a less definite way and without bitterness,
seeing before them a long life in which they
could not miss attaining happiness.

Maria stole an occasional glance at Eutrope Gagnon, but she quickly turned away,
for she always surprised his humbly worshipping eyes. For a year she had become used
to his frequent visits, nor felt displeasure when
every Sunday evening added to the family
circle this brown face that was continually so
patient and good-humoured; but the short absence of a month had not left things the same,
for she had brought home to the fireside an
undefined feeling that a page of her life was
turned, in which he would have no share.

The ordinary subjects of conversation ex-
hausted, they played cards: *quatre-sept* and
boeuf; then Eutrope looked at his big silver
watch and said that it was time to be going.
His lantern lit, the good-byes said, he halted
on the threshold for a moment to observe
the night.

"It is raining!" he exclaimed.

His hosts made toward the door to see for themselves; the rain had in truth begun, a spring rain with great drops that fell heavily, under which the snow was already softening and melting.

"The sou'east has taken hold," announced the elder Chapdelaine. "Now we can say that the winter is practically over."

Everyone had his own way of expressing relief and delight; but it was Maria who stood longest by the door, hearkening to the sweet patter of the rain, watching the indistinct movement of cloud in the dark sky above the darker mass of the forest, breathing the mild air that came from the south.

"Spring is not far . . . Spring is not far . . ."

In her heart she felt that never since the earth began was there a springtime like this springtime to-be.

CHAPTER III

FRANÇOIS PASSES BY

CHAPTER III

FRANÇOIS PASSES BY

ONE morning three days later, on opening the door, Maria's ear caught a sound that made her stand motionless and listening. The distant and continuous thunder was the voice of wild waters, silenced all winter by the frost.

"The ice is going out," she announced to those within. "You can hear the falls."

This set them all talking once again of the opening season, and of the work soon to be commenced. The month of May came in with alternate warm rains and fine sunny days which gradually conquered the accumulated ice and snow of the long winter. Low stumps and roots were beginning to appear, although the shade of close-set cypress and fir prolonged the death-struggle of the perishing snow-drifts; the roads became quagmires; wherever the brown mosses were uncovered they were full of water as a sponge. In other lands it was already spring; vigorously the sap was running, buds were bursting and presently leaves would unfold; but the soil of far northern Canada must be rid of one chill and heavy mantle before clothing itself afresh in green.

A dozen times in the course of the day Maria and her mother opened the window to feel the softness of the air, listen to the tinkle of water running from the last drifts on higher slopes, or hearken to the mighty roar telling that the exulting Peribonka was free, and hurrying to the lake a freight of ice-floes from the remote north.

Chapdelaine seated himself that evening on the door-step for his smoke; a stirring of memory brought the remark:—"François will soon be passing. He said that perhaps he would come to see us." Maria replied with a scarce audible "Yes," and blessed the shadow hiding her face.

Ten days later he came, long after night-fall. The women were alone in the house with Tit'Bé and the children, the father having gone for seed-grain to Honfleur whence he would only return on the morrow. Telesphore and Alma Rose were asleep,

[48]

Tit'Bé was having a last pipe before the family prayer, when Chien barked several times and got up to sniff at the closed door. Then two light taps were heard. The visitor waited for the invitation before he entered and stood before them.

His excuses for so late a call were made without touch of awkwardness. "We are camped at the end of the portage above the rapids. The tent had to be pitched and things put in order to make the Belgians comfortable for the night. When I set out I knew it was hardly the hour for a call and that the paths through the woods must be pretty bad. But I started all the same, and when I saw your light . ."

His high Indian boots were caked with mud to the knee; he breathed a little deeply between words, like a man who has been running; but his keen eyes were quietly confident.

"Only Tit'Bé has changed," said he. "When you left Mistassini he was but so high . . ." With a hand he indicated the stature of a child. Mother Chapdelaine's face was bright with interest; doubly pleased

[49]

to receive a visitor and at the chance of talking about old times.

"Nor have you altered in these seven years;
not a bit; as for Maria . . . surely you find
a difference!"

He gazed at Maria with something of
wonder in his eyes. "You see that . . . that
I saw her the other day at Peribonka."
Tone and manner showed that the meeting
of a fortnight ago had been allowed to blot
the remoter days from his recollection. But
since the talk was of her he ventured an
appraising glance.

Her young vigour and health, the beautiful
heavy hair and sunburnt neck of a country
girl, the frank honesty of eye and gesture,
all these things, thought he, were possessions
of the child of seven years ago; and twice
or thrice he shook his head as though to
say that, in truth, she had not changed.
But the consciousness too was there that he,
if not she, had changed, for the sight of her
before him took strange hold upon his heart.

Maria's smile was a little timid, but soon
she dared to raise her eyes and look at him
in turn. Assuredly a handsome fellow; comely

of body, revealing so much of supple strength;
comely of face in well-cut feature and fearless eye . . . To herself she said with some
surprise that she had not thought him thus—
more forward perhaps, talking freely and
rather positively—but now he scarcely spoke
at all and everything about him had an air
of perfect simplicity. Doubtless it was his
expression that had given her this idea, and
his bold straightforward manner.

Mother Chapdelaine took up her questioning:—"And so you sold the farm when your
father died, François?"

"Yes, I sold everything. I was never a
very good hand at farming, you know.
Working in the shanties, trapping, making
a little money from time to time as a guide
or in trade with the Indians, that is the life
for me; but to scratch away at the same
fields from one year's end to another, and
stay there forever, I would not have been
able to stick to that all my life; I would
have felt like a cow tethered to a stake."

"That is so, some men are made that way.
Samuel, for example, and you, and many
another. It seems as if the woods had some

magic for you . . ." She shook her head and looked at him in wonderment. "Frozen in winter, devoured by flies in summer; living in a tent on the snow, or in a log cabin full of chinks that the wind blows through, you like that better than spending your life on a good farm, near shops and houses. Just think of it; a nice bit of level land without a stump or a hollow, a good warm house all papered inside, fat cattle pasturing or in the stable; for people well stocked with implements and who keep their health, could there be anything better or happier?"

François Paradis looked at the floor without making answer, perhaps a trifle ashamed of these wrong-headed tastes of his. "A fine life for those who are fond of the land," he said at last, "but I should never have been content."

It was the everlasting conflict between the types: pioneer and farmer, the peasant from France who brought to new lands his ideals of ordered life and contented immobility, and that other in whom the vast wilderness awakened distant atavistic instincts for wandering and adventure.

Accustomed for fifteen years to hear her mother vaunting the idyllic happiness of the farmer in the older settlements, Maria had very naturally come to believe that she was of the same mind; now she was no longer certain about it. But whoever was right she well knew that not one of the well-to-do young fellows at St. Prime, with his Sunday coat of fine cloth and his fur collar, was the equal of François Paradis in muddy boots and faded woollen jersey.

Replying to further questions he spoke of his journeys on the North Shore and to the head-waters of the rivers—of it all very naturally and with a shade of hesitation, scarcely knowing what to tell and what to leave out, for the people he was speaking to lived in much the same kind of country and their manner of life was little different.

"Up there the winters are harder yet than here, and still longer. We have only dogs to draw our sleds, fine strong dogs, but bad-tempered and often half wild, and we feed them but once a day, in the evening, on frozen fish. . . . Yes, there are settlements, but almost no farming; the men live by trap-

[53]

ping and fishing . . . No, I never had any
difficulty with the Indians; I always got on
very well with them.   I know nearly all those
on the Mistassini and this river, for they used
to come to our place before my father died.
You see he often went trapping in winter when
he was not in the shanties, and one season
when he was at the head of the Rivière aux
Foins, quite alone, a tree that he was cutting
for firewood slipped in falling, and it was the
Indians who found him by chance next day,
crushed and half-frozen though the weather
was mild. He was in their game preserve,
and they might very well have pretended
not to see him and have left him to die there;
but they put him on their toboggan, brought
him to their camp, and looked after him.
You knew my father: a rough man who
often took a glass, but just in his dealings,
and with a good name for doing that sort of
thing himself. So when he parted with these
Indians he told them to stop and see him in
the spring when they would be coming down
to Pointe Bleue with their furs:—'François
Paradis of Mistassini,' said he to them,
'will not forget what you have done . . .

[54]

François Paradis.' And when they came in spring while running the river he looked after them well and every one carried away a new ax, a fine woollen blanket and tobacco for six months. Always after that they used to pay us a visit in the spring, and father had the pick of their best skins for less than the companies' buyers had to pay. When he died they treated me in the same way because I was his son and bore the same name, François Paradis. With more capital I could have made a good bit of money in this trade—a good bit of money."

He seemed a little uncomfortable at having talked so much, and arose to go. "We shall be coming down in a few weeks and I will try to stay a little longer," he said as he departed. "It is good to see you again."

On the door-step his keen eyes sought in Maria's for something that he might carry into the depth of the green woods whither he was bent; but they found no message. In her maidenly simplicity she feared to show herself too bold, and very resolutely she kept her glance lowered, like the young girls with richer parents who return from the

convents in Chicoutimi trained to look on
the world with a superhuman demureness.

Scarcely was François gone when the two
women and Tit'Bé knelt for the evening
prayer. The mother led in a high voice,
speaking very rapidly, the others answering
in a low murmur. Five Paters, five Aves,
the Acts, and then a long responsive Litany.

"Holy Mary, mother of God, pray for us
now and at the hour of our death . . ."

"Immaculate heart of Jesus, have pity on
us . . ."

The window was open and through it came
the distant roaring of the falls. The first
mosquitos of the spring, attracted by the
light, entered likewise and the slender music
of their wings filled the house. Tit'Bé went
and closed the window, then fell on his knees
again beside the others.

"Great St. Joseph, pray for us . . ."

"St. Isidore, pray for us . . ."

The prayers over, mother Chapdelaine
sighed out contentedly:—"How pleasant it
is to have a caller, when we see hardly anyone but Eutrope Gagnon from year's end
to year's end. But that is what comes of

living so far away in the woods . . . Now, when I was a girl at St. Gedeon, the house was full of visitors nearly every Saturday evening and all Sunday: Adelard Saint-Onge who courted me for such a long time; Wilfrid Tremblay, the merchant, who had nice manners and was always trying to speak as the French do; many others as well— not counting your father who came to see us almost every night for three years, while I was making up my mind . . ."

Three years! Maria thought to herself that she had only seen François Paradis twice since she was a child, and she felt ashamed at the beating of her heart.

CHAPTER IV
WILD LAND

CHAPTER IV

WILD LAND

AFTER a few chilly days, June suddenly brought veritable spring weather. A blazing sun warmed field and forest, the lingering patches of snow vanished even in the deep shade of the woods; the Peribonka rose and rose between its rocky banks until the alders and the roots of the nearer spruces were drowned; in the roads the mud was incredibly deep. The Canadian soil rid itself of the last traces of winter with a semblance of mad haste, as though in dread of another winter already on the way.

Esdras and Da'Bé returned from the shanties where they had worked all the winter. Esdras was the eldest of the family, a tall fellow with a huge frame, his face bronzed, his hair black; the low forehead and prominent chin gave him a Neronian profile, domineering, not without a suggestion of brutality; but he spoke softly, measuring his words, and was endlessly patient. In face alone had he anything of the tyrant; it was as though the long rigours of the climate and the fine sense and good humour of the race had refined his heart to a simplicity and kindliness that his formidable aspect seemed to deny.)

Da'Bé, also tall, was less heavily built and more lively and merry. He was like his father.

The married couple had given their first children, Esdras and Maria, fine, high-sounding, sonorous names; but they had apparently wearied of these solemnities, for the next two children never heard their real names pronounced; always had they been called by the affectionate diminutives of childhood, Da'Bé and Tit'Bé. With the last pair, however, there had been a return to the earlier ceremonious manner:—Telesphore . . . Alma Rose.

"When the boys get back we are going to make land," the father had promised. And, with the help of Edwige Légaré, their hired man, they set about the task.

In the Province of Quebec there is much uncertainty in the spelling and the use of names. A scattered people in a huge half-

wild country, unlettered for the most part
and with no one to turn to for counsel but
the priests, is apt to pay attention only to
the sound of names, caring nothing about
their appearance when written or the sex
to which they pertain. Pronunciation has
naturally varied in one mouth or another,
in this family or that, and when a formal
occasion calls for writing, each takes leave
to spell his baptismal name in his own way,
without a passing thought that there may
be a canonical form. Borrowings from other
languages have added to the uncertainties
of orthography and gender. Individuals sign
indifferently, Denise, Denije or Deneije;
Conrad or Courade; men bear such names
as Hermenegilde, Aglaë, Edwige.

Edwige Légaré had worked for the Chapdelaines these eleven summers. That is to
say, for wages of twenty dollars a month he
was in harness each day from four in the
morning till nine at night at any and every
job that called for doing, bringing to it a sort
of frenzied and inexhaustible enthusiasm;
for he was one of those men incapable by
his nature of working save at the full pitch

of strength and energy, in a series of berserk
rages. Short and broad, his eyes were the
brightest blue—a thing rare in Quebec—at
once piercing and guileless, set in a visage
the colour of clay that always showed cruel
traces of the razor, topped by hair of nearly
the same shade. With a pride in his appearance that was hard to justify he shaved
himself two or three times a week, always in
the evening, before the bit of looking-glass
that hung over the pump and by the feeble
light of the little lamp—driving the steel
through his stiff beard with groans that
showed what it cost him in labour and
anguish. Clad in shirt and trousers of brown-
ish homespun, wearing huge dusty boots,
he was from head to heel of a piece with the
soil, nor was there aught in his face to re-
deem the impression of rustic uncouthness.

Chapdelaine, his three sons and man, proceeded then to "make land." The forest
still pressed hard upon the buildings they
had put up a few years earlier: the little
square house, the barn of planks that gaped
apart, the stable built of blackened logs and
chinked with rags and earth. Between the

scanty fields of their clearing and the darkly
encircling woods lay a broad stretch which
the ax had but half-heartedly attacked. A
few living trees had been cut for timber, and
the dead ones, sawn and split, fed the great
stove for a whole winter; but the place was
a rough tangle of stumps and interlacing
roots, of fallen trees too far rotted to burn,
of others dead but still erect amid the alder
scrub.

Thither the five men made their way one
morning and set to work at once, without a
word, for every man's task had been settled
beforehand.

The father and Da'Bé took their stand face
to face on either side of a tree, and their axes,
helved with birch, began to swing in rhythm.
At first each hewed a deep notch, chopping
steadily at the same spot for some seconds,
then the ax rose swiftly and fell obliquely on
the trunk a foot higher up; at every stroke a
great chip flew, thick as the hand, splitting
away with the grain. When the cuts were
nearly meeting, one stopped and the other
slowed down, leaving his ax in the wood for
a moment at every blow; the mere strip, by

some miracle still holding the tree erect,
yielded at last, the trunk began to lean and
the two axmen stepped back a pace and
watched it fall, shouting at the same instant
a warning of the danger.

It was then the turn of Edwige Legaré and
Esdras; when the tree was not too heavy
each took an end, clasping their strong hands
beneath the trunk, and then raised themselves—backs straining, arms cracking under
the stress—and carried it to the nearest
heap with short unsteady steps, getting over
the fallen timber with stumbling effort.
When the burden seemed too heavy, Tit'Bé
came forward leading Charles Eugene dragging a tug-bar with a strong chain; this was
passed round the trunk and fastened, the
horse bent his back, and with the muscles
of his hindquarters standing out, hauled
away the tree which scraped along the stumps
and crushed the young alders to the ground.

At noon Maria came out to the door-step
and gave a long call to tell them that dinner
was ready. Slowly they straightened up
among the stumps, wiping away with the
backs of their hands the drops of sweat that

ran into their eyes, and made their way to
the house.

Already the pea-soup smoked in the plates.
The five men set themselves at table without
haste, as if sensation were somewhat dulled
by the heavy work; but as they caught their
breath a great hunger awoke, and soon they
began to eat with keen appetite. The two
women waited upon them, filling the empty
plates, carrying about the great dish of pork
and boiled potatoes, pouring out the hot
tea. When the meat had vanished the diners
filled their saucers with molasses in which
they soaked large pieces of bread; hunger
was quickly appeased, because they had
eaten fast and without a word, and then
plates were pushed back and chairs tilted
with sighs of satisfaction, while hands were
thrust into pockets for their pipes, and the
pigs' bladders bulging with tobacco.

Edwige Légaré, seating himself on the
door-step, proclaimed two or three times:—
"I have dined well . . . I have dined well
. . ." with the air of a judge who renders
an impartial decision; after which he leaned
against the post and let the smoke of his

pipe and the gaze of his small light-coloured
eyes pursue the same purposeless wander-
ings. The elder Chapdelaine sank deeper
and deeper into his chair, and ended by falling asleep; the others smoked and chatted
about their work.

"If there is anything," said the mother,
"which could reconcile me to living so far
away in the woods, it is seeing my men-folk
make a nice bit of land—a nice bit of land
that was all trees and stumps and roots,
which one beholds in a fortnight as bare as
the back of your hand, ready for the plough;
surely nothing in the world can be more
pleasing or better worth doing." The rest
gave assent with nods, and were silent for a
while, admiring the picture. Soon however
Chapdelaine awoke, refreshed by his sleep
and ready for work; then all arose and went
out together.

The place where they had worked in the
morning was yet full of stumps and over-
grown with alders. They set themselves to
cutting and uprooting the alders, gathering
a sheaf of branches in the hand and severing
them with the ax, or sometimes digging the

earth away about the roots and tearing up
the whole bush together. The alders dis-
posed of, there remained the stumps.

Légaré and Esdras attacked the smaller
ones with no weapons but their axes and
stout wooden prizes. They first cut the roots
spreading on the surface, then drove a lever
well home, and, chests against the bar, threw
all their weight upon it. When their efforts
could not break the hundred ties binding the
tree to the soil Légaré continued to bear
heavily that he might raise the stump a little,
and while he groaned and grunted under the
strain Esdras hewed away furiously level
with the ground, severing one by one the
remaining roots.

A little distance away the other three men
handled the stumping-machine with the aid
of Charles Eugene. The pyramidal scaffold-
ing was put in place above a large stump and
lowered, the chains which were then at-
tached to the root passed over a pulley, and
the horse at the other end started away
quickly, flinging himself against the traces
and showering earth with his hoofs. A short
and desperate charge, a mad leap often

arrested after a few feet as by the stroke of
a giant fist; then the heavy steel blades
would swing up anew, gleaming in the sun,
and fall with a dull sound upon the stubborn
wood, while the horse took breath for a
moment, awaiting with excited eye the word
that would launch him forward again. And
afterwards there was still the labour of
hauling or rolling the big stumps to the
pile—at fresh effort of back, of soil-stained
hands with swollen veins, and stiffened arms
that seemed grotesquely striving with the
heavy trunk and the huge twisted roots.

The sun dipped toward the horizon, disappeared; the sky took on softer hues above
the forest's dark edge, and the hour of supper
brought to the house five men of the colour
of the soil.

While waiting upon them Madame Chapdelaine asked a hundred questions about the
day's work, and when the vision arose before
her of this patch of land they had cleared,
superbly bare, lying ready for the plough,
her spirit was possessed with something of a
mystic's rapture.

With hands upon her hips, refusing to seat

herself at table, she extolled the beauty of the world as it existed for her: not the beauty wherein human beings have no hand, which the townsman makes such an ado about with his unreal ecstasies—mountains lofty and bare, wild seas—but the quiet unaffected loveliness of the level champaign, finding its charm in the regularity of the long furrow and the sweetly-flowing stream—the naked champaign courting with willing abandon the fervent embraces of the sun.

She sang the great deeds of the four Chapdelaines and Edwige Légaré, their struggle against the savagery of nature, their triumph of the day. She awarded praises and displayed her own proper pride, albeit the five men smoked their wooden or clay pipes in silence, motionless as images after their long task; images of earthy hue, hollow-eyed with fatigue.

"The stumps are hard to get out," at length said the elder Chapdelaine, "the roots have not rotted in the earth so much as I should have imagined. I calculate that we shall not be through for three weeks." He glanced questioningly at Légaré who gravely confirmed him.

"Three weeks . . . Yes, confound it! That is what I think too."

They fell silent again, patient and determined, like men who face a long war.

The Canadian spring had but known a few weeks of life when, by calendar, the summer was already come; it seemed as if the local weather god had incontinently pushed the season forward with august finger to bring it again into accord with more favoured lands to the south. For torrid heat fell suddenly upon them, heat well-nigh as unmeasured as was the winter's cold. The tops of the spruces and cypresses, forgotten by the wind, were utterly still, and above the frowning outline stretched a sky bare of cloud which likewise seemed fixed and motionless. From dawn till nightfall a merciless sun calcined the ground.

The five men worked on unceasingly, while from day to day the clearing extended its borders by a little; deep wounds in the uncovered soil showed the richness of it.

Maria went forth one morning to carry them water. The father and Tit'Bé were cutting alders, Da'Bé and Esdras piled the

cut trees. Edwige Légaré was attacking a
stump by himself; a hand against the trunk,
he had grasped a root with the other as one
seizes the leg of some gigantic adversary in
a struggle, and he was fighting the combined
forces of wood and earth like a man furious
at the resistance of an enemy. Suddenly the
stump yielded and lay upon the ground; he
passed a hand over his forehead and sat
down upon a root, running with sweat, overcome by the exertion. When Maria came
near him with her pail half full of water,
the others having drunk, he was still seated,
breathing deeply and saying in a bewildered
way:—"I am done for . . . Ah! I am done
for." But he pulled himself together on
seeing her, and roared out:—"Cold water!
Perdition! Give me cold water."

Seizing the bucket he drank half its con-
tents and poured the rest over his head and
neck; still dripping, he threw himself afresh
upon the vanquished stump and began to
roll it toward a pile as one carries off a prize.

Maria stayed for a few moments looking
at the work of the men and the progress they
had made, each day more evident, then hied

her back to the house swinging the empty
bucket, happy to feel herself alive and well
under the bright sun, dreaming of all the
joys that were to be hers, nor could be long
delayed if only she were earnest and patient
enough in her prayers.

Even at a distance the voices of the men
came to her across the surface of the ground
baked by the heat; Esdras, his hands beneath a young jack pine, was saying in his
quiet tones:—"Gently . . . together now!"

Légaré was wrestling with some new inert
foe, and swearing in his half-stifled way:—
"Perdition! I'll make you stir, so I will."
His gasps were nearly as audible as the words.
Taking breath for a second he rushed once
more into the fray, arms straining, wrench-
ing with his great back. And yet again his
voice was raised in oaths and lamentations:
—"I tell you that I'll have you . . . Oh
you rascal! Isn't it hot? . . . I'm pretty
nearly finished . . ." His complaints ripened
into one mighty cry:—"Boss! We are going
to kill ourselves making land."

Old Chapdelaine's voice was husky but
still cheerful as he answered: "Tough!

Edwige, tough! The pea-soup will soon be ready."

And in truth it was not long before Maria, once more on the door-step, shaping her hands to carry the sound, sent forth the ringing call to dinner.

Toward evening a breeze arose and a delicious coolness fell upon the earth like a pardon. But the sky remained cloudless.

"If the fine weather lasts," said mother Chapdelaine, "the blueberries will be ripe for the feast of Ste. Anne."

CHAPTER V
THE VOWS

CHAPTER V

THE VOWS

HE fine weather continued, and early in July the blueberries were ripe.

Where the fire had passed, on rocky slopes, wherever the woods were thin and the sun could penetrate, the ground had been clad in almost unbroken pink by the laurel's myriad tufts of bloom; at first the reddening blueberries contended with them in glowing colour, but under the constant sun these slowly turned to pale blue, to royal blue, to deepest purple, and when July brought the feast of Ste. Anne the bushes laden with fruit were broad patches of violet amid the rosy masses now beginning to fade.

The forests of Quebec are rich in wild berries; cranberries, Indian pears, black currants, sarsaparilla spring up freely in the wake of the great fires, but the blueberry, the bilberry or whortleberry of France, is of all the most abundant and delicious.

The gathering of them, from July to September, is an industry for many families who spend the whole day in the woods; strings of children down to the tiniest go swinging their tin pails, empty in the morning, full and heavy by evening. Others only gather the blueberries for their own use, either to make jam or the famous pies national to French Canada.

Two or three times in the very beginning of July Maria, with Telesphore and Alma Rose, went to pick blueberries; but their day had not come, and the gleanings barely sufficed for a few tarts of proportions to excite a smile.

"On the feast of Ste. Anne," said their mother by way of consolation, "we shall all go a-gathering; the men as well, and whoever fails to bring back a full pail is not to have any."

But Saturday, the eve of Ste. Anne's day, was memorable to the Chapdelaines; an evening of company such as their house in the forest had never seen.

When the men returned from work Eutrope Gagnon was already there. He had

supped, he said, and while the others were
at their meal he sat by the door in the cooler
air that entered, balancing his chair on two
legs. The pipes going, talk naturally turned
toward the labours of the soil, and the care
of stock.

"With five men," said Eutrope, "you
have a good bit of land to show in a short
while. But working alone, as I do, without
a horse to draw the heavy logs, one makes
poor headway and has a hard time of it. However you are always getting on, getting on."

Madame Chapdelaine, liking him, and
feeling a great sympathy for his solitary
labour in this worthy cause, gave him a few
words of encouragement. "You don't make
very quick progress by yourself, that is true
enough, but a man lives on very little when
he is alone, and then your brother Egide will
be coming back from the drive with two or
three hundred dollars at least, in time for
the hay-making and the harvest, and, if you
both stay here next winter, in less than two
years you will have a good farm."

Assenting with a nod, his glance found
Maria, as though drawn thither by the thought

that in two years, fortune favouring, he might hope . . .

"How does the drive go?" asked Esdras. "Is there any news from that quarter?"

"I had word through Ferdina Larouche, a son of Thadée Larouche of Honfleur, who got back from La Tuque last month. He said that things were going well; the men were not having too bad a time."

The shanties, the drive, these are the two chief heads of the great lumbering industry, even of greater importance for the Province of Quebec than is farming. From October till April the axes never cease falling, while sturdy horses draw the logs over the snow to the banks of the frozen rivers; and, when spring comes, the piles melt one after another into the rising waters and begin their long adventurous journey through the rapids. At every abrupt turn, at every fall, where logs jam and pile, must be found the strong and nimble river-drivers, practised at the dangerous work, at making their way across the floating timber, breaking the jams, aiding with ax and pike-pole the free descent of this moving forest.

"A hard time!" exclaimed Légaré with scorn. "The young fellows of to-day don't know the meaning of the words. After three months in the woods they are in a hurry to get home and buy yellow boots, stiff hats and cigarettes, and to go and see their girls. Even in the shanties, as things are now, they are as well fed as in a hotel, with meat and potatoes all winter long. Now, thirty years ago . . ."

He broke off for a moment, expressing with a shake of his head those prodigious changes that the years had wrought.

"Thirty years ago, when the railway from Quebec was built, I was there; that was something like hardship, I can tell you! I was only sixteen years of age but I chopped with the rest of them to clear the right of way, always twenty-five miles ahead of the steel, and for fourteen months I never clapped eye on a house. We had no tents, summer or winter, only shelters of boughs that we made for ourselves, and from morning till night it was chop, chop, chop,—eaten by the flies, and in the course of the same day soaked with rain and roasted by the sun."

[83]

"Every Monday morning they opened a sack of flour and we made ourselves a bucketful of pancakes, and all the rest of the week, three times a day, one dug into that pail for something to eat. By Wednesday, no longer any pancakes, because they were all stuck together; nothing there but a mass of dough. One cut off a big chunk of dough with one's knife, put that in his belly, and then chopped and chopped again!"

"When we got to Chicoutimi where provisions could reach us by water we were worse off than Indians, pretty nearly naked, all scratched and torn, and I well remember some who began to cry when told they could go home, because they thought they would find all their people dead, so long had the time seemed to them. Hardship! That was hardship if you like."

"That is so," said Chapdelaine, "I can recall those days. Not a single house on the north side of the lake: no one but Indians and a few trappers who made their way up here in summer by canoe and in winter with dog-sleds, much as it is now in the Labrador."

[84]

The young folk were listening keenly to these tales of former times. "And now," said Esdras, "here we are fifteen miles beyond the lake, and when the Roberval boat is running we can get to the railway in twelve hours."

They meditated upon this for a while without a word, contrasting past and present; the cruel harshness of life as once it was, the easy day's journey now separating them from the marvels of the iron way, and the thought of it filled them with naïve wonder.

All at once Chien set up a low growl; the sound was heard of approaching footsteps. "Another visitor!" Madame Chapdelaine announced in a tone mingling pleasure and astonishment.

Maria also arose, agitated, smoothing her hair with unconscious hand; but it was Ephrem Surprenant of Honfleur who opened the door.

"We have come to pay you a visit!" He shouted this with the air of one who announces a great piece of news. Behind him was someone unknown to them, who bowed and smiled in a very mannerly way.

"My nephew Lorenzo," was Ephrem Surprenant's introduction, "a son of my brother Elzéar who died last autumn. You never met him, it is a long time since he left this country for the States."

They were quick to find a chair for the young man from the States, and the uncle undertook the duty of establishing the nephew's genealogy on both sides of the house, and of setting forth his age, trade and the particulars of his life, in obedience to the Canadian custom. "Yes, a son of my brother Elzéar who married a young Bourglouis of Kiskisink. You should be able to recall that, Madame Chapdelaine?"

From the depths of her memory mother Chapdelaine unearthed a number of Surprenants and as many Bourglouis, and gave the list with their baptismal names, successive places of residence and a full record of their alliances.

"Right. Precisely right. Well, this one here is Lorenzo. He has been in the States for many years, working in a factory."

Frankly interested, everyone took another good look at Lorenzo Surprenant. His face

was rounded, with well-cut features, eyes
gentle and unwavering, hands white; with
his head a little on one side he smiled ami-
ably, neither superior nor embarrassed under
this concentrated gaze.

"He came here," continued his uncle, "to
settle affairs after the death of Elzéar, and
to try to sell the farm."

"He has no wish to hold on to the land
and cultivate it?" questioned the elder
Chapdelaine.

Lorenzo Surprenant's smile broadened and
he shook his head. "No, the idea of settling
down on the farm does not tempt me, not in
the least. I earn good wages where I am and like
the place very well; I am used to the work."

He checked himself, but it was plain that
after the kind of life he had been living and
what he had seen of the world, existence on
a farm between a humble little village and
the forest seemed a thing insupportable.

"When I was a girl," said mother Chapdelaine, "pretty nearly everyone went off
to the States. Farming did not pay as well
as it does now, prices were low, we were
always hearing of the big wages earned over

there in the factories, and every year one family after another sold out for next to nothing and left Canada. Some made a lot of money, no doubt of that, especially those families with plenty of daughters; but now it is different and they are not going as once they did . . . So you are selling the farm?"

"Yes, there has been some talk with three Frenchmen who came to Mistook last month. I expect we shall make a bargain."

"And are there many Canadians where you are living? Do the people speak French?"

"At the place I went to first, in the State of Maine, there were more Canadians than Americans or Irish; everyone spoke French; but where I live now, in the State of Massachusetts, there are not so many. A few families however; we call on one another in the evenings."

"Samuel once thought of going West," said Madame Chapdelaine, "but I was never willing. Among people speaking nothing but English I should have been unhappy all the rest of my days. I used to say to him:— 'Samuel, we Canadians are always better off among Canadians.'"

When the French Canadian speaks of himself it is invariably and simply as a "Canadian"; whereas for all the other races that followed in his footsteps, and peopled the country across to the Pacific, he keeps the name of origin: English, Irish, Polish, Russian; never admitting for a moment that the children of these, albeit born in the country, have an equal title to be called "Canadians." Quite naturally, and without thought of offending, he appropriates the name won in the heroic days of his forefathers.

"And is it a large town where you are?"

"Ninety thousand," said Lorenzo with a little affectation of modesty.

"Ninety thousand! Bigger than Quebec!"

"Yes, and we are only an hour by train from Boston. A really big place, that."

And he set himself to telling of the great American cities and their magnificence, of the life filled with ease and plenty, abounding in refinements beyond imagination, which is the portion of the well paid artisan.

In silence they listened to his words. Framed in the open door-way the last crim-

son of the sky, fading to paler tints, rose
above the vague masses of the forest,—a
column resting upon its base. The mosquitos began to arrive in their legions, and the
humming of innumerable wings filled the
clearing with low continuous sound.

"Telesphore," directed the father, "make
us a smudge. Take the old tin pail." Telesphore covered the bottom of the leaky vessel
with earth, filling it then with dry chips and
twigs which he set ablaze. When the flame
was leaping up brightly he returned with an
armful of herbs and leaves and smothered it;
the volume of stinging smoke which ascended
was carried by the wind into the house and
drove out the countless horde. At length
they were at peace, and with sighs of relief
could desist from the warfare. The very last
mosquito settled on the face of little Alma
Rose. With great seriousness she pronounced
the ritual words:—"Fly, fly, get off my face,
my nose is not a public place!" Then she
made a swift end of the creature with a slap.
The smoke drifted obliquely through the
door-way; within the house, no longer stirred
by the breeze, it spread in a thin cloud; the

walls became indistinct and far-off; the group seated between door and stove resolved into a circle of dim faces hanging in a white haze.

"Greetings to everyone!" The tones rang clear, and François Paradis, emerging from the smoke, stood upon the threshold. For weeks Maria had been expecting him. Half an hour earlier the sound of a step without had sent the blood to her cheek, and yet the arrival of him she awaited moved her with joyous surprise.

"Offer your chair, Da'Bé!" cried mother Chapdelaine. Four callers from three different quarters converging upon her, truly nothing more was needed to fill her with delightful excitement. An evening indeed to be remembered!

"There! You are forever saying that we are buried in the woods and see no company," triumphed her husband. "Count them over: eleven grown-up people!" Every chair in the house was filled; Esdras, Tit'Bé and Eutrope Gagnon occupied the bench, Chapdelaine, a box turned upside down; from the step Telesphore and Alma Rose watched the mounting smoke.

"And look," said Ephrem Surprenant, "how many young fellows and only one girl!" The young men were duly counted: three Chapdelaines, Eutrope Gagnon, Lorenzo Surprenant, François Paradis. As for the one girl . . . Every eye was turned upon Maria, who smiled feebly and looked down, confused.

"Had you a good trip, François?—He went up the river with strangers to buy furs from the Indians," explained Chapdelaine; who presented to the others with formality—"François Paradis, son of François Paradis from St. Michel de Mistassini." Eutrope Gagnon knew him by name, Ephrem Surprenant had met his father:—"A tall man, taller still than he, of a strength not to be matched." It only remained to account for Lorenzo Surprenant,—"who has come home from the States"—and all the conventions had been honoured.

"A good trip," answered François. "No, not very good. One of the Belgians took a fever and nearly died. After that it was rather late in the season; many Indian families had already gone down to Ste.

Anne de Chicoutimi and could not be found;
and on top of it all a canoe was wrecked
when running a rapid on the way back, and
it was hard work fishing the pelts out of the
river, without mentioning the fact that one
of the bosses was nearly drowned,—the same
one that had the fever. No, we were unlucky all through. But here we are none
the less, and it is always another job over
and done with." A gesture signified to the
listeners that the task was completed, the
wages paid and the ultimate profits or losses
not his affair.

"Always another job over and done
with,"—he slowly repeated the words. "The
Belgians were in a hurry to reach Peribonka
on Sunday, to-morrow; but, as they had
another man, I left them to finish the journey
without me so that I might spend the evening with you. It does one's heart good to
see a house again."

His glance strayed contentedly over the
meager smoke-filled interior and those who
peopled it. In the circle of faces tanned by
wind and sun, his was the brownest and
most weather-beaten; his garments showed

many rents, one side of the torn woollen
jersey flapped upon his shoulder, moccasins
replaced the long boots he had worn in the
spring. He seemed to have brought back
something of nature's wildness from the
head-waters of the rivers where the Indians
and the great creatures of the woods find
sanctuary. And Maria, whose life would
not allow her to discern the beauty of that
wilderness because it lay too near her, yet
felt that some strange charm was at work
and was throwing its influence about her.

Esdras had gone for the cards; cards with
faded red backs and dog-eared corners,
where the lost queen of hearts was replaced
by a square of pink cardboard bearing the
plainly-written legend *dame de cœur*. They
played at *quatre-sept*. The two Surprenants,
uncle and nephew, had Madame Chapdelaine and Maria for partners; after each
game the beaten couple left the table and
gave place to two other players. Night had
fallen; some mosquitos made their way
through the open window and went hither
and thither with their stings and irritating
music.

"Telesphore!" called out Esdras, "see to the smudge, the flies are coming in." In a few minutes smoke pervaded the house again, thick, almost stifling, but greeted with delight. The party ran its quiet course. An hour of cards, some talk with a visitor who bears news from the great world, these are still accounted happiness in the Province of Quebec.

Between the games, Lorenzo Surprenant entertained Maria with a description of his life and his journeyings; in turn asking questions about her. He was far from putting on airs, yet she felt disconcerted at finding so little to say, and her replies were halting and timid.

The others talked among themselves or watched the play. Madame recalled the many gatherings at St. Gedeon in the days of her girlhood, and looked from one to the other, with unconcealed pleasure at the fact that three young men should thus assemble beneath her roof. But Maria sat at the table devoting herself to the cards, and left it for some vacant seat near the door with scarcely a glance about her. Lorenzo Surprenant was always by her side and talking; she felt the continual regard of Eutrope Gagnon with that familiar look of patient waiting; she was conscious of the handsome bronzed face and fearless eyes of François Paradis who sat very silent beyond the door, elbows on his knees.

"Maria is not at her best this evening," said Madame Chapdelaine by way of excusing her, "she is really not used to having visitors you see . . ." Had she but known! . . .

Four hundred miles away, at the far headwaters of the rivers, those Indians who have held aloof from missionaries and traders are squatting round a fire of dry cypress before their lodges, and the world they see about them, as in the earliest days, is filled with dark mysterious powers: the giant Wendigo pursuing the trespassing hunter; strange potions, carrying death or healing, which wise old men know how to distil from roots and leaves; incantations and every magic art. And here on the fringe of another world, but a day's journey from the railway, in this wooden house filled with acrid smoke,

[96]

another all-conquering spell, charming and
bewildering the eyes of three young men, is
being woven into the shifting cloud by a
sweet and guileless maid with downcast eyes.

· The hour was late; the visitors departed;
first the two Surprenants, then Eutrope
Gagnon, only François Paradis was left,—
standing there and seeming to hesitate.

"You will sleep here to-night, François?"
asked the father.

His wife heard no reply. "Of course!"
said she. "And to-morrow we will all gather
blueberries. It is the feast of Ste. Anne."

When a few moments later François
mounted to the loft with the boys, Maria's
heart was filled with happiness. This seemed
to bring him a little nearer, to draw him
within the family circle.

The morrow was a day of blue sky, a day
when from the heavens some of the sparkle
and brightness descends to earth. The green
of tender grass and young wheat was of a
ravishing delicacy, even the dun woods
borrowed something from the azure of the
sky.

François came down in the morning looking a different man, in clothes borrowed from Da'Bé and Esdras, and after he had shaved and washed Madame Chapdelaine complimented him on his appearance.

When breakfast was over and the hour of the mass come, all told their chaplet together; and then the long delightful idle Sunday lay before them. But the day's programme was already settled. Eutrope Gagnon came in just as they were finishing dinner, which was early, and at once they all set forth, provided with pails, dishes and tin mugs of every shape and size.

The blueberries were fully ripe. In the burnt lands the purple of the clusters and the green of the leaves now overcame the paling rose of the laurels. The children began picking at once with cries of delight, but their elders scattered through the woods in search of the larger patches, where one might sit on one's heels and fill a pail in an hour. The noise of footsteps on dry twigs, of rustling in the alder bushes, the calls of Telesphore and Alma Rose to one another, all faded slowly into the distance, and about each gatherer was only the buzzing of flies drunk with sunshine, and the voice of the wind in the young birches and aspens.

"There is a fine clump over here," said a voice. Maria's heart beat faster as she arose and went toward François Paradis who was kneeling behind the alders. Side by side they picked industriously for a time, then plunged farther into the woods, stepping over fallen trees, looking about them for the deep blue masses of the ripe berries.

"There are very few this year," said François. "It was the spring frosts that killed the blossoms." He brought to the berry-seeking his woodsman's knowledge. "In the hollows and among the alders the snow was lying longer and kept them from freezing."

They sought again and made some happy finds: broad clumps of bushes laden with huge berries which they heaped into their pails. In the space of an hour these were filled; they rose and went to sit on a fallen tree to rest themselves.

Mosquitos swarmed and circled in the fervent afternoon heat. Every moment the hand must be raised to scatter them; after a panic-stricken flight they straightway re-

turned, reckless and pitiless, bent only on
finding one tiny spot to plant a sting; with
their sharp note was blended that of the
insatiate black-fly, filling the woods with un-
ceasing sound. Living trees there were not
many; a few young birches, some aspens,
alder bushes were stirring in the wind among
the rows of lifeless and blackened trunks.

François Paradis looked about him as
though to take his bearings. "The others
cannot be far away," he said.

"No," replied Maria in a low voice. But
neither he nor she called to summon them.

A squirrel ran down the bole of a dead
birch tree and watched the pair with his
sharp eyes for some moments before ventur-
ing to earth. The strident flight of heavy
grasshoppers rose above the intoxicated
clamour of the flies; a wandering air brought
the fall's dull thunder through the alders.

François Paradis stole a glance at Maria,
then turned his eyes away and tightly clasped
his hands. Ah, but she was good to look
upon! Thus to sit beside her, to catch
these shy glimpses of the strong bosom, the
sweet face so modest and so patient, the

utter simplicity of attitude and of her rare gestures; a great hunger for her awoke in him, and with it a new and marvellous tenderness, for he had lived his life with other men, in hard give-and-take, among the wild forests and on the snowy plains.

Well he knew she was one of those women who, giving themselves, give wholly, reckoning not the cost; love of body and of soul, strength of arm in the daily task, the unmeasured devotion of a spirit that does not waver. So precious the gift appeared to him that he dared not ask it.

"I am going down to Grand'Mère next week," he said, almost in a whisper, "to work on the lumber-dam. But I will never take a glass, not one, Maria!" Hesitating a moment he stammered out, eyes on the ground: "Perhaps . . . they have said something against me?"

"No."

"It is true that I used to drink a bit, when I got back from the shanties and the drive; but that is all over now. You see when a young fellow has been working in the woods for six months, with every kind of hardship

and no amusement, and gets out to La Tuque
or Jonquières with all the winter's wages in
his pocket, pretty often he loses his head; he
throws his money about and sometimes takes
too much . . . But that is all over."

"And it is also true that I used to swear.
When one lives all the time with rough men
in the woods or on the rivers one gets the
habit. Once I swore a good deal, and the
curé, Mr. Tremblay, took me to task because I said before him that I wasn't afraid
of the devil. But there is an end of that too,
Maria. All the summer I am to be working
for two dollars and a half a day and you
may be sure that I shall save money. And
in the autumn there will be no trouble finding a job as foreman in a shanty, with big
wages. Next spring I shall have more than
five hundred dollars saved, clear, and I shall
come back. . . ."

Again he hesitated, and the question he
was about to put took another form upon
his lips. "You will be here still . . . next
spring?"

"Yes."

And after the simple question and simpler

answer they fell silent and so long remained, wordless and grave, for they had exchanged their vows.

CHAPTER VI
THE STUFF OF DREAMS

CHAPTER VI

THE STUFF OF DREAMS

IN July the hay was maturing, and by the middle of August it was only a question of awaiting a few dry days to cut and store it. But after many weeks of fine weather the frequent shifts of wind which are usual in Quebec once more ruled the skies.

Every morning the men scanned the heavens and took counsel together. "The wind is backing to the sou'east. Bad luck! Beyond question it will rain again," said Edwige Légaré with a gloomy face. Or it was old Chapdelaine who followed the movement of the white clouds that rose above the tree-tops, sailed in glad procession across the clearing, and disappeared behind the dark spires on the other side.

"If the nor'west holds till to-morrow we shall begin," he announces. But next day the wind had backed afresh, and the cheerful clouds of yesterday, now torn and shapeless, straggling in disorderly rout, seemed to be fleeing like the wreckage of a broken army.

Madame Chapdelaine foretold inevitable misfortune. "Mark my words, we shall not have good hay-making weather. They say that down by the end of the lake some people of the same parish have gone to law with one another. Of a certainty the good God does not like that sort of thing!"

Yet the Power at length was pleased to show indulgence, and the north-west wind blew for three days on end, steady and strong, promising a rainless week. The scythes were long since sharpened and ready, and the five men set to work on the morning of the third day. Légaré, Esdras and the father cut; Da'Bé and Tit'Bé followed close on their heels, raking the hay together. Toward evening all five took their forks in hand and made it into cocks, high and carefully built, lest a change of wind should bring rain. But the sunshine lasted. For five days they carried on, swinging the scythe steadily from right to left with that broad free movement that seems so easy to the practised hand, and is in truth the hardest to learn

[108]

and the most fatiguing of all the labours known to husbandry.

Flies and mosquitos rose in swarms from the cut hay, stinging and tormenting the workers; a blazing sun scorched their necks, and smarting sweat ran into their eyes; when evening came, such was the ache of backs continually bent, they could not straighten themselves without making wry faces. Yet they toiled from dawn to nightfall without loss of a second, hurrying their meals, feeling nothing but gratitude and happiness that the weather stood fair.

Three or four times a day Maria or Telesphore brought them a bucket of water which they stood in a shady spot to keep it cool; and when throats became unbearably dry with heat, exertion and the dust of the hay, they went by turns to swallow great draughts and deluge wrists or head.

In five days all the hay was cut, and, the drought persisting, on the morning of the sixth day they began to break and scatter the cocks they intended lodging in the barn before night. The scythes had done their work and the forks came into play. They

threw down the cocks, spread the hay in the
sun, and toward the end of the afternoon,
when dry, heaped it anew in piles of such a
size that a man could just lift one with a
single motion to the level of a well-filled
hay-cart.

Charles Eugene pulled gallantly between
the shafts; the cart was swallowed up in the
barn, stopped beside the mow, and once
again the forks were plunged into the hard-
packed hay, raised a thick mat of it with
strain of wrist and back, and unloaded it to
one side. By the end of the week the hay,
well-dried and of excellent colour, was all
under cover; the men stretched themselves
and took long breaths, knowing the fight
was over and won.

"It may rain now if it likes," said Chapdelaine. "It will be all the same to us." But
it appeared that the sunshine had not been
timed with exact relation to their peculiar
needs, for the wind held in the north-west
and fine days followed one upon the other
in unbroken succession.

The women of the Chapdelaine household
had no part in the work of the fields. The

father and his three tall sons, all strong and
skilled in farm labour, could have managed
everything by themselves; if they continued
to employ Légaré and to pay him wages it
was because he had entered their service
eleven years before, when the children were
young, and they kept him now, partly
through habit, partly because they were loth
to lose the help of so tremendous a worker.
During the hay-making then, Maria and her
mother had only their usual tasks: house-
work, cooking, washing and mending, the
milking of three cows and the care of the
hens, and once a week the baking which
often lasted well into the night.

On the eve of a baking Telesphore was
sent to hunt up the bread-pans which
habitually found their way into all corners
of the house and shed—being in daily use to
measure oats for the horse or Indian corn
for the fowls, not to mention twenty other
casual purposes they were continually serv-
ing. By the time all were routed out and
scrubbed the dough was rising, and the
women hastened to finish other work that
their evening watch might be shortened.

Telesphore made a blazing fire below the oven with branches of gummy cypress that smelled of resin, then fed it with tamarack logs, giving a steady and continuous heat. When the oven was hot enough, Maria slipped in the pans of dough; after which nothing remained but to tend the fire and change the position of the pans as the baking required.

Too small an oven had been built five years before, and ever since then the family did not escape a weekly discussion about the new oven it was imperative to construct, which unquestionably should have been put in hand without delay; but on each trip to the village, by one piece of bad luck and another, someone forgot the necessary cement; and so it happened that the oven had to be filled two or even three times to make weekly provision for the nine mouths of the household.

Maria invariably took charge of the first baking; invariably too, when the oven was ready for the second batch of bread and the evening well advanced, her mother would say considerately:—"You can go to bed,

Maria, I will look after the second baking."
And Maria would reply never a word,
knowing full well that the mother would
presently stretch herself on the bed for a
little nap and not awake till morning. She
then would revive the smudge that smoul-
dered every evening in the damaged tin pail,
install the second batch of bread, and seat
herself upon the door-step, her chin resting
in her hands, upheld through the long hours
of the night by her inexhaustible patience.

Twenty paces from the house the clay
oven with its sheltering roof of boards
loomed dark, but the door of the fireplace
fitted badly and one red gleam escaped
through the chink; the dusky border of the
forest stole a little closer in the night.
Maria sat very still, delighting in the quiet
and the coolness, while a thousand vague
dreams circled about her like a flock of
wheeling birds.

There was a time when this night-watch
passed in drowsiness, as she resignedly
awaited the moment when the finished task
would bring her sleep; but since the coming
of François Paradis the long weekly vigil

was very sweet to her, for she could think
of him and of herself with nothing to distract
her dear imaginings. Simple they were,
these thoughts of hers, and never did they
travel far afield. In the springtime he will
come back; this return of his, the joy of
seeing him again, the words he will say when
they find themselves once more alone, the
first touch of hands and lips. Not easy was
it for Maria to make a picture for herself
of how these things were to come about.

Yet she essayed. First she repeated his
full name two or three times, formally, as
others spoke it: François Paradis, from St.
Michel de Mistassini . . . François Paradis . . . Then suddenly, with sweet in-
timacy,—François!

The evocation fails not. He stands before
her tall and strong, bold of eye, his face
bronzed with sun and snow-glare. He is by
her side, rejoicing at the sight of her, rejoicing that he has kept his faith, has lived
the whole year discreetly, without drinking
or swearing. There are no blueberries yet
to gather—it is only springtime—yet some
good reason they find for rambling off to

the woods; he walks beside her without word
or joining of hands, through the massed
laurel flaming into blossom, and naught beyond does either need to flush the cheek,
to quicken the beating of the heart.

Now they are seated upon a fallen tree,
and thus he speaks: "Were you lonely without me, Maria?" Most surely it is the first
question he will put to her; but she is able
to carry the dream no further for the sudden
pain stabbing her heart. Ah! dear God!
how long will she have been lonely for him
before that moment comes! A summer to
be lived through, an autumn, and all the endless winter! She sighs, but the steadfast
patience of the race sustains her, and her
thoughts turn upon herself and what the
future may be holding.

When she was at St. Prime, one of her
cousins who was about to be wedded spoke
often to her of marriage. A young man
from the village and another from Normandin had both courted her; for long months
spending the Sunday evenings together at
the house.

"I was fond of them both,"—thus she de-

clared to Maria. "And I really think I liked
Zotique best; but he went off to the drive on
the St. Maurice, and he wasn't to be back
till summer; then Romeo asked me and I
said, 'Yes.' I like him very well, too."

Maria made no answer, but even then her
heart told her that all marriages are not like
that; now she is very sure. The love of
François Paradis for her, her love for him, is
a thing apart—a thing holy and inevitable—
for she was unable to imagine that between
them it should have befallen otherwise; so
must this love give warmth and unfading colour to every day of the dullest life. Always
had she dim consciousness of such a presence
—moving the spirit like the solemn joy of
chanted masses, the intoxication of a sunny
windy day, the happiness that some unlooked-
for good fortune brings, the certain promise
of abundant harvest . . .

In the stillness of the night the roar of the
fall sounds loud and near; the north-west
wind sways the tops of spruce and fir with a
sweet cool sighing; again and again, farther
away and yet farther, an owl is hooting; the
chill that ushers in the dawn is still remote.

And Maria, in perfect contentment, rests upon the step, watching the ruddy beam from her fire—flickering, disappearing, quickened again to birth.

She seems to remember someone long since whispering in her ear that the world and life were cheerless and gray. The daily round, brightened only by a few unsatisfying, fleeting pleasures; the slow passage of unchanging years; the encounter with some young man, like other young men, whose patient and hopeful courting ends by winning affection; a marriage then, and afterwards a vista of days under another roof, but scarce different from those that went before. So does one live, the voice had told her. Naught very dreadful in the prospect, and, even were it so, what possible but submission; yet all level, dreary and chill as an autumn field.

It is not true! Alone there in the darkness Maria shakes her head, a smile upon her lips, and knows how far from true it is. When she thinks of François Paradis, his look, his bearing, of what they are and will be to one another, he and she, something within her bosom has strange power to burn with the

[117]

touch of fire, and yet to make her shiver. All
the strong youth of her, the long-suffering of
her sooth-fast heart find place in it; in the
upspringing of hope and of longing, this vision
of her approaching miracle of happiness.

Below the oven the red gleam quivers and
fails.

"The bread must be ready!" she murmurs
to herself. But she cannot bring herself at
once to rise, loth as she is to end the fair
dream that seems only beginning.

CHAPTER VII

A MEAGER REAPING

CHAPTER VII

A MEAGER REAPING

EPTEMBER arrived, and the dryness so welcome for the hay-making persisted till it became a disaster. According to the Chapdelaines, never had the country been visited with such a drought as this, and every day a fresh motive was suggested for the divine displeasure.

Oats and wheat took on a sickly colour ere attaining their growth; a merciless sun withered the grass and the clover aftermath, and all day long the famished cows stood lowing with their heads over the fences. They had to be watched continually, for even the meager standing crop was a sore temptation, and never a day went by but one of them broke through the rails in the attempt to appease her hunger among the grain.

Then, of a sudden one evening, as though weary of a constancy so unusual, the wind shifted and in the morning came the rain. It fell off and on for a week, and when it ceased and the wind hauled again to the north-west, autumn had come.

The autumn! And it seemed as though spring were here but yesterday. The grain was yet unripe, though yellowed by the drought; nothing save the hay was in barn; the other crops could draw nutriment from the soil only while the too brief summer warmed it, and already autumn was here, the forerunner of relentless winter, of the frosts, and soon the snows . . .

Between the wet days there was still fine bright weather, hot toward noon, when one might fancy that all was as it had been: the harvest still unreaped, the changeless setting of spruces and firs, and ever the same sunsets of gray and opal, opal and gold, and skies of misty blue above the same dark woodland. But in the mornings the grass was sometimes white with rime, and swiftly followed the earliest dry frosts which killed and blackened the tops of the potatoes.

Then, for the first time, a film of ice appeared upon the drinking-trough; melted by the afternoon sun it was there a few days later, and yet a third time in the same week.

Frequent changes of wind brought an alterna-
tion of mild rainy days and frosty mornings;
but every time the wind came afresh from the
north-west it was a little colder, a little more
remindful of the icy winter blasts. Everywhere is autumn a melancholy season,
charged with regrets for that which is
departing, with shrinking from what is to
come; but under the Canadian skies it is
sadder and more moving than elsewhere, as
though one were bewailing the death of a
mortal summoned untimely by the gods
before he has lived out his span.

Through the increasing cold, the early
frosts, the threats of snow, they held back
their hands and put off the reaping from day
to day, encouraging the meager grain to steal
a little nourishment from the earth's failing
veins and the spiritless sun. At length, harvest they must, for October approached.
About the time when the leaves of birches and
aspens were turning, the oats and the wheat
were cut and carried to the barn under a
cloudless sky, but without rejoicing.

The yield of grain was poor enough, yet the
hay-crop had been excellent, so that the year

as a whole gave occasion neither for excess of joy nor sorrow. However, it was long before the Chapdelaines, in evening talk, ceased deploring the unheard-of August droughts, the unprecedented September frosts, which betrayed their hopes. Against the miserly shortness of the summer and the harshness of a climate that shows no mercy they did not rebel, were even without a touch of bitterness; but they did not give up contrasting the season with that other year of wonders which fond imagination made the standard of their comparisons; and thus was ever on their lips the countryman's perpetual lament, so reasonable to the ear, but which recurs unfailingly: "Had it only been an ordinary year!"

CHAPTER VIII
ENTRENCHED AGAINST WINTER

CHAPTER VIII
ENTRENCHED AGAINST WINTER

ONE October morning Maria's first
vision on arising was of countless
snow-flakes sifting lazily from the
skies. The ground was covered,
the trees white; verily it seemed
that autumn was over, when in
other lands it had scarce begun.

But Edwige Légaré thus pronounced sentence: "After the first snowfall there is yet a
month before winter sets in. The old folks
always so declared, and I believe it myself."
He was right; for in two days a rain carried
off the snow and the dark soil again lay bare.
Still the warning was heeded, and they set
about preparations; the yearly defences
against the snow that may not be trifled with,
and the piercing cold.

Esdras and Da'Bé protected the foundation
of their dwelling with earth and sand, making
an embankment at the foot of the walls; the
other men, armed with hammer and nails,
went round the outside of the house, nailing

up, closing chinks, remedying as best they could the year's wear and tear. Within, the women forced rags into the crevices, pasted upon the wainscotting at the north-west side old newspapers brought from the village and carefully preserved, tested with their hands in every corner for draughts.

These things accomplished, the next task was to lay in the winter's store of wood. Beyond the fields, at the border of the forest plenty of dead trees yet were standing. Esdras and Légaré took ax in hand and felled for three days; the trunks were piled, awaiting another fall of snow when they could be loaded on the big wood-sleigh.

All through October, frosty and rainy days came alternately, and meanwhile the woods were putting on a dress of unearthly loveliness. Five hundred paces from the Chapdelaine house the bank of the Peribonka fell steeply to the rapid water and the huge blocks of stone above the fall, and across the river the opposite bank rose in the fashion of a rocky amphitheatre, mounting to loftier heights—an amphitheatre trending in a vast curve to the northward. Of the birches, aspens, alders and wild cherries scattered upon the slope, October made splashes of many-tinted red and gold. Throughout these weeks the ruddy brown of mosses, the change-less green of fir and cypress, were no more than a background, a setting only for the ravishing colours of those leaves born with the spring, that perish with the autumn. The wonder of their dying spread over the hills and unrolled itself, an endless riband following the river, ever as beautiful, as rich in shades brilliant and soft, as enrapturing, when they passed into the remoteness of far northern regions and were unseen by human eye.

But ere long there sweeps from out the cold north a mighty wind like a final sentence of death, the cruel ending to a reprieve, and soon the poor leaves, brown, red and golden, shaken too unkindly, strow the ground; the snow covers them, and the white expanse has only for adornment the sombre green of trees that alter not their garb—triumphing now, as do those women inspired with bitter wisdom who barter their right to beauty for life everlasting.

In November Esdras, Da'Bé and Edwige

Légaré went off again to the shanties. The
father and Tit'Bé harnessed Charles Eugene
to the wood-sleigh, and laboured at hauling in
the trees that had been cut, and piling them
near the house; that done, the two men took
the double-handed saw and sawed, sawed,
sawed from morning till night; it was then the
turn of the axes, and the logs were split as
their size required. Nothing remained but to
cord the split wood in the shed beside the
house, where it was sheltered from the snow;
the huge piles mingling the resinous cypress
which gives a quick hot flame, spruce and red
birch, burning steadily and longer, close-
grained white birch with its marble-like
surface, slower yet to be consumed and leaving red embers in the morning after a long
winter's night.

The moment for laying in wood is also that
of the slaughtering. After entrenching against
cold comes the defence against hunger. The
quarters of pork went into the brine-tub; from
a beam in the shed there hung the side of a
fat heifer—the other half sold to people in
Honfleur—which the cold would keep fresh
till spring; sacks of flour were piled in a corner

of the house, and Tit'Bé, provided with a spool of brass wire, set himself to making nooses for hares.

After the bustle of summer they relapsed into easy-going ways, for the summer is painfully short and one must not lose a single hour of those precious weeks when it is possible to work on the land, whereas the winter drags slowly and gives all too much time for the tasks it brings.

The house became the centre of the universe; in truth the only spot where life could be sustained, and more than ever the great cast-iron stove was the soul of it. Every little while some member of the family fetched a couple of logs from under the staircase; cypress in the morning, spruce throughout the day, in the evening birch, pushing them in upon the live coals. Whenever the heat failed, mother Chapdelaine might be heard saying anxiously:—"Don't let the fire out, children." Whereupon Maria, Tit'Bé or Telesphore would open the little door, glance in and hasten to the pile of wood.

In the mornings Tit'Bé jumped out of bed long before daylight to see if the great sticks

of birch had done their duty and burned all
night; should, unluckily, the fire be out he
lost no time in rekindling it with birch-bark
and cypress branches, placed heavier pieces
on the mounting flame, and ran back to
snuggle under the brown woollen blankets and
patchwork quilt till the comforting warmth
once more filled the house.

Outside, the neighbouring forest, and even
the fields won from it, were an alien unfriendly
world, upon which they looked wonderingly
through the little square windows. And sometimes this world was strangely beautiful in
its frozen immobility, with a sky of flawless
blue and a brilliant sun that sparkled on the
snow; but the immaculateness of the blue and
the white alike was pitiless and gave hint of
the murderous cold.

Days there were when the weather was
tempered and the snow fell straight from the
clouds, concealing all; the ground and the low
growth was covered little by little, the dark
line of the woods was hidden behind the
curtain of serried flakes. Then in the morning
the sky was clear again, but the fierce north-
west wind swayed the heavens. Powdery

snow, whipped from the ground, drove across
the burnt lands and the clearings in blinding
squalls, and heaped itself behind whatever
broke the force of the gale. To the south-east
of the house it built an enormous cone, and
between house and stable raised a drift five
feet high through which the shovel had to
carve a path; but to windward the ground was
bare, scoured by the persistent blast.

On such days as these the men scarcely left
the house except to care for the beasts, and
came back on the run, their faces rasped with
the cold and shining-wet with snow-crystals
melted by the heat of the house. Chapdelaine
would pluck the icicles from his moustache,
slowly draw off his sheepskin-lined coat and
settle himself by the stove with a satisfied
sigh. "The pump is not frozen?" he asks.
"Is there plenty of wood in the house?"

Assured that the frail wooden fortress is
provided with water, wood and food, he gives
himself up to the indolences of winter quarters, smoking pipes innumerable while the
women-folk are busy with the evening meal.
The cold snaps the nails in the plank walls
with reports like pistol-shots; the stove

crammed with birch roars lustily; the howling of the wind without is like the cries of a besieging host.

"It must be a bad day in the woods!" thinks Maria to herself; and then perceives that she has spoken aloud.

"In the woods they are better off than we are here," answers her father. "Up there where the trees stand close together one does not feel the wind. You can be sure that Esdras and Da'Bé are all right."

"Yes?"

But it was not of Esdras and Da'Bé that she had just been thinking.

CHAPTER IX

ONE THOUSAND AVES

CHAPTER IX

ONE THOUSAND AVES

SINCE the coming of winter they had often talked at the Chapdelaines about the holidays, and now these were drawing near.

"I am wondering whether we shall have any callers on New Year's Day," said Madame Chapdelaine one evening. She went over the list of all relatives and friends able to make the venture. "Azalma Larouche does not live so far away, but she—she is not very energetic. The people at St. Prime would not care to take the journey. Possibly Wilfrid or Ferdinand might drive from St. Gedeon if the ice on the lake were in good condition." A sigh disclosed that she still was dreaming of the coming and going in the old parishes at the time of the New Year, the family dinners, the unlooked-for visits of kindred arriving by sleigh from the next village, buried under rugs and furs, behind a horse whose coat was white with frost.

Maria's thoughts were turning in another direction. "If the roads are as bad as they were last year," said she, "we shall not be able to attend the midnight mass. And yet I should so much have liked it this time, and father promised . . . "

Through the little window they looked on the gray sky, and found little to cheer them. To go to midnight mass is the natural and strong desire of every French-Canadian peasant, even of those living farthest from the settlements. What do they not face to accomplish it! Arctic cold, the woods at night, obliterated roads, great distances do but add to the impressiveness and the mystery. This anniversary of the birth of Jesus is more to them than a mere fixture in the calendar with rites appropriate; it signifies the renewed promise of salvation, an occasion of deep rejoicing, and those gathered in the wooden church are imbued with sincerest fervour, are pervaded with a deep sense of the supernatural. This year, more than ever, Maria yearned to attend the mass after many weeks of remoteness from houses and from churches; the favours she would fain demand seemed more likely to be granted were she able to prefer them before the altar, aided in heavenward flight by the wings of music.

But toward the middle of December much snow fell, dry and fine as dust, and three days before Christmas the north-west wind arose and made an end of the roads. On the morrow of the storm Chapdelaine harnessed Charles Eugene to the heavy sleigh and departed with Tit'Bé; they took shovels to clear the way or lay out another route. The two men returned by noon, worn out, white with snow, asserting that there would be no breaking through for several days. The disappointment must be borne; Maria sighed, but the idea came to her that there might be other means of attaining the divine goodwill.

"Is it true, mother," she asked as evening was falling, "that if you repeat a thousand Aves on the day before Christmas you are always granted the thing you seek?"

"Quite true," her mother reverently answered. "One desiring a favour who says her thousand Aves properly before midnight on Christmas Eve, very seldom fails to receive what she asks."

On Christmas Eve the weather was cold but
windless. The two men went out betimes in
another effort to beat down the road, with no
great hope of success; but long before they
left, and indeed long before daylight, Maria
began to recite her Aves. Awakening very
early, she took her rosary from beneath the
pillow and swiftly repeated the prayer, passing from the last word to the first without
stopping, and counting, bead by bead.

The others were still asleep; but Chien left
his place at the stove when he saw that she
moved, and came to sit beside the bed,
gravely reposing his head upon the coverings.
Maria's glance wandered over the long white
muzzle resting upon the brown wool, the
liquid eyes filled with the dumb creature's
pathetic trustfulness, the drooping glossy
ears; while she ceased not to murmur
the sacred words:—"Hail Mary, full of
grace   .   .   ."

Soon Tit'Bé jumped from bed to put wood
upon the fire; an impulse of shyness caused
Maria to turn away and hide her rosary under
the coverlet as she continued to pray. The
stove roared; Chien went back to his usual

spot, and for another half-hour nothing was
stirring in the house save the fingers of Maria
numbering the boxwood beads, and her lips as
they moved rapidly in the task she had laid
upon herself.

Then must she arise, for the day was dawn-
ing; make the porridge and the pancakes
while the men went to the stable to care for
the animals, wait upon them when they
returned, wash the dishes, sweep the house.
What time she attended to these things,
Maria was ever raising a little higher toward
heaven the monument of her Aves; but the
rosary had to be laid aside and it was hard
to keep a true reckoning. As the morning
advanced however, no urgent duty calling,
she was able to sit by the window and
steadily pursue her undertaking.

Noon; and already three hundred Aves.
Her anxiety lessens, for now she feels almost
sure of finishing in time. It comes to her mind
that fasting would give a further title to heavenly consideration, and might, with reason,
turn hopes into certainties; wherefore she ate
but little, foregoing all those things she liked
the best.

[141]

Throughout the afternoon she must knit the woollen garment designed for her father as a New Year's gift, and though the faithful repetition ceased not, the work of her fingers was something of a distraction and a delay; then came the long preparations for supper, and finally Tit'Bé brought his mittens to be mended, so all this time the Aves made slow and impeded progress, like some devout procession brought to halt by secular interruption.

But when it was evening and the tasks of the day were done, she could resume her seat by the window where the feeble light of the lamp did not invade the darkness, look forth upon the fields hidden beneath their icy cloak, take the rosary once more in her hands and throw her heart into the prayer. She was happy that so many Aves were left to be recited, since labour and difficulty could only add merit to her endeavour; even did she wish to humble herself further and give force to her prayer by some posture that would bring uneasiness and pain, by some chastening of the flesh.

Her father and Tit'Bé smoked, their feet against the stove; her mother sewed new ties to old moose-hide moccasins. Outside, the moon had risen, flooding the chill whiteness with colder light, and the heavens were of a marvellous purity and depth, sown with stars that shone like that wondrous star of old.

"Blessed art Thou amongst women . . ."

Through repeating the short prayer often-times and quickly she grew confused and sometimes stopped, her dazed mind lost among the well-known words. It is only for a moment; sighing she closes her eyes, and the phrase which rises at once to her memory and her lips ceases to be mechanical, detaches itself, again stands forth in all its hallowed meaning.

"Blessed art Thou amongst women . . ."

At length a heaviness weighs upon her, and the holy words are spoken with greater effort and slowly; yet the beads pass through her fingers in endless succession, and each one launches the offering of an Ave to that sky where Mary the compassionate is surely seated on her throne, hearkening to the music of prayers that ever rise, and brooding over the memory of that blest night.

"The Lord is with Thee . . ."

The fence-rails were very black upon the white expanse palely lighted by the moon; trunks of birch trees standing against the dark background of forest were like the skeletons of living creatures smitten with the cold and stricken by death; but the glacial night was awesome rather than affrighting.

"With the roads as they are we will not be the only ones who have to stay at home this evening," said Madame Chapdelaine. "But is there anything more lovely than the midnight mass at Saint Coeur de Marie, with Yvonne Boilly playing the harmonium, and Pacifique Simard who sings the Latin so beautifully!" She was very careful to say nothing that might seem reproachful or complaining on such a night as this, but in spite of herself the words and tone had a sad ring of loneliness and remoteness. Her husband noticed it, and, himself under the influence of the day, was quick to take the blame.

"It is true enough, Laura, that you would have had a happier life with some other man than me, who lived on a comfortable farm, near the settlements."

"No, Samuel; what the good God does is always right. I grumble . . . Of course I grumble. Is there anyone who hasn't something to grumble about? But we have never been unhappy, we two; we have managed to live without faring over-badly; the boys are fine boys, hard-working, who bring us nearly all they earn; Maria too is a good girl . . ."

Affected by these memories of the past, they also were thinking of the candles already lit, of the hymns soon to be raised in honour of the Saviour's birth. Life had always been a simple and a straightforward thing for them; severe but inevitable toil, a good understanding between man and wife, obedience alike to the laws of nature and of the Church. Everything was drawn into the same woof; the rites of their religion and the daily routine of existence so woven together that they could not distinguish the devout emotion possessing them from the mute love of each for each.

Little Alma Rose heard praises in the air and hastened to demand her portion. "I have been a good girl too, haven't I, father?"

"Certainly . . . Certainly. A black sin indeed if one were naughty on the day when the little Jesus was born."

To the children, Jesus of Nazareth was ever "the little Jesus," the curly-headed babe of the sacred picture; and in truth, for the parents as well, such was the image oftenest brought to mind by the Name. Not the sad enigmatic Christ of the Protestant, but a being more familiar and less august, a new-born infant in his mother's arms, or at least a tiny child who might be loved without great effort of the mind or any thought of the coming sacrifice.

"Would you like me to rock you?"

"Yes."

He took the little girl on his knees and began to swing her back and forth.

"And are we going to sing too?"

"Yes."

"Very well; now sing with me:"

> Dans son étable,
> Que Jésus est charmant!
> Qu'il est aimable
> Dans son abaissement . . .

He began in quiet tones that he might not drown the other slender voice; but soon emo-

tion carried him away and he sang with all his
might, his gaze dreamy and remote. Telesphore drew near and looked at him with
worshipping eyes. To these children brought
up in a lonely house, with only their parents
for companions, Samuel Chapdelaine embod-
ied all there was in the world of wisdom and
might. As he was ever gentle and patient,
always ready to take the children on his knee
and sing them hymns, or those endless old
songs he taught them one by one, they loved
him with a rare affection.

> . . . Tous les palais des rois
> N'ont rien de comparable
> Aux beautés que je vois
> Dans cette étable.

"Once more? Very well."

This time the mother and Tit'Be joined in.
Maria could not resist staying her prayers for
a few moments that she might look and hearken; but the words of the hymn renewed her
ardour, and she soon took up the task again
with a livelier faith . . . "Hail Mary, full
of grace . . ."

> Trois gros navires sont arrivés,
> Charges d'avoine, chargés de blé.
> Nous irons sur l'eau nous y prom-promener,
> Nous irons jouer dans l'île . . .

"And now? Another song: which?" Without waiting for a reply he struck in . . .

"No? not that one . . . *Claire Fontaine?* Ah! That's a beautiful one, that is! We shall all sing it together."

He glanced at Maria, but seeing the beads ever slipping through her fingers he would not intrude.

A la claire fontaine
M'en allant promener,
J'ai trouvé l'eau si belle
Que je m'y suis baigné . . .
Il y a longtemps que je t'aime,
Jamais je ne t'oublierai. . .

Words and tune alike haunting; the unaffected sadness of the refrain lingering in the ear, a song that well may find its way to any heart.

. . Sur la plus haute branche,
Le rossignol chantait.
Chante, rossignol, chante,
Toi qui a le cœur gai . . .
Il y a longtemps que je t'aime
Jamais je ne t'oublierai . . .

The rosary lay still in the long fingers. Maria did not sing with the others; but she was listening, and this lament of a love that was unhappy fell very sweetly and movingly on her spirit a little weary with prayer.

. . . Tu as le cœur à rire,
Moi je l'ai à pleurer,
J'ai perdu ma maîtresse
Sans pouvoir la r'trouver,
Pour un bouquet de roses
Que je lui refusai
Il y a longtemps que je t'aime,
Jamais je ne t'oublierai.

Maria looked through the window at the white fields circled by mysterious forest; the passion of religious feeling, the tide of young love rising within her, the sound of the familiar voices, fused in her heart to a single emotion. Truly the world was filled with love that evening, with love human and divine, simple in nature and mighty in strength, one and the other most natural and right; so intermingled that the beseeching of heavenly favour upon dear ones was scarcely more than the expression of an earthly affection, while the artless love songs were chanted with solemnity of voice and exaltation of spirit fit for addresses to another world.

. . Je voudrais que la rose
Fût encore au rosier,
Et que le rosier même
A la mer fût jeté.
Il y a longtemps, que je t'aime,
Jamais je ne t'oublierai . .

[149]

"Hail Mary, full of grace . . ."

The song ended, Maria forthwith resumed her prayers with zeal refreshed, and once again the tale of the Aves mounted.

Little Alma Rose, asleep on her father's knee, was undressed and put to bed; Telesphore followed; Tit'Bé arose in turn, stretched himself, and filled the stove with green birch logs; the father made a last trip to the stable and came back running, saying that the cold was increasing. Soon all had retired, save Maria.

"You won't forget to put out the lamp?"

"No, father."

Forthwith she quenched the light, preferring it so, and seated herself again by the window to repeat the last Aves. When she had finished, a scruple assailed her, and a fear lest she had erred in the reckoning, because it had not always been possible to count the beads of her rosary. Out of prudence she recited yet another fifty and then was silent— jaded, weary, but full of happy confidence, as though the moment had brought her a promise inviolable.

The world outside was lit; wrapped in that frore splendour which the night unrolls over lands of snow when the sky is clear and the moon is shining. Within the house was darkness, and it seemed that wood and field had illumined themselves to signal the coming of the holy hour.

"The thousand Aves have been said," murmured Maria to herself, "but I have not yet asked for anything . . . not in words." She had thought that perhaps it were not needful; that the Divinity might understand without hearing wishes shaped by lips—Mary above all . . . Who had been a woman upon earth. But at the last her simple mind was taken with a doubt, and she tried to find speech for the favour she was seeking.

François Paradis . . . Most surely it concerns François Paradis. Hast Thou already guessed it, O Mary, full of grace? How might she frame this her desire without impiety? That he should be spared hardship in the woods . . . That he should be true to his word and give up drinking and swearing . . . That he return in the spring . . .

That he return in the spring . . . She goes no further, for it seems to her that when he is with her again, his promise kept, all the

happiness in the world must be within their
reach, unaided . . . almost unaided . . .
If it be not presumptuous so to think . . .

That he return in the spring . . . Dreaming of his return, of François, the handsome
sunburnt face turned to hers, Maria forgets
all else, and looks long with unseeing eyes at
the snow-covered ground which the moonlight
has turned into a glittering fabric of ivory and
mother-of-pearl—at the black pattern of the
fences outlined upon it, and the menacing
ranks of the dark forest.

CHAPTER X
STRAYING TRACKS

CHAPTER X

STRAYING TRACKS

NEW YEAR'S DAY, and not a single caller! Toward evening the mother of the family, a trifle cast down, hid her depression behind a mask of extra cheeriness. "Even if no one comes," said she, "that is no reason for allowing ourselves to be unhappy. We are going to make *la tire*."

The children exclaimed with delight, and followed the preparations with impatient eyes. Molasses and brown sugar were set on the stove to boil, and when this had proceeded far enough Telesphore brought in a large dish of lovely white snow. They all gathered about the table as a few drops of the boiling syrup were allowed to fall upon the snow where they instantly became crackly bubbles, deliciously cold.

Each was helped in turn, the big people making a merry pretence of the children's unfeigned greed; but soon, and very wisely, the tasting was checked, that appetite might not be in peril for the real *la tire*, the confection of which had only begun. After further cooking, and just at the proper moment, the cooling toffee must be pulled for a long time. The mother's strong hands plied unceasingly for five minutes, folding and drawing out the sugary skein; the movement became slower and slower, until, stretched for the last time to the thickness of a finger, it was cut into lengths with scissors—not too easily, for it was already hard. The *la tire* was made.

The children were busy with their first portions, when a knocking was heard on the door. "Eutrope Gagnon," at once declared Chapdelaine. "I was just saying to myself that it would be an odd thing if he did not come and spend the evening with us."

Eutrope Gagnon it was in truth. Entering, he bade them all good evening, and laid his woollen cap upon the table. Maria looked at him, a blush upon her cheek. Custom ordains that on the first day of the year the young men shall kiss the women-folk, and Maria knew well enough that Eutrope, shy as he was, would exercise his privilege; she stood motionless by the table, unprotesting, yet thinking of another kiss she would have dearly welcomed. But the young man took the chair offered him and sat down, his eyes upon the floor.

"You are the only visitor who has come our way to-day," said Chapdelaine, "and I suppose you have seen no one either. I felt pretty certain you would be here this evening."

"Naturally . . . I would not let New Year's Day go by without paying you a visit. But, besides that, I have news to tell."

"News?"

Under the questioning eyes of the household he did not raise his eyes.

"By your face I am afraid you have bad news."

"Yes."

With a start of fear the mother half rose. "Not about the boys?"

"No, Madame Chapdelaine. Esdras and Da'Bé are well, if that be God's pleasure. The word I bring is not of them—not of your own kin. It concerns a young man you know." Pausing a moment he spoke a name under his breath:—"François Paradis."

His glance was lifted to Maria and as quickly fell, but she did not so much as see his look of honest distress. Deep stillness weighed upon the house—upon the whole universe. Everything alive and dead was breathlessly awaiting news of such dreadful moment—touching him that was for her the one man in all the world . . .

"This is what happened. You knew perhaps that he was foreman in a shanty above La Tuque, on the Vermilion River. About the middle of December he suddenly told the boss that he was going off to spend Christmas and New Year at Lake St. John—up here. The boss objected, naturally enough; for if the men take ten or fifteen days' leave right in the middle of the winter you might as well stop the work altogether. The boss did not wish him to go and said so plainly; but you know François—a man not be thwarted when a notion entered his head. He answered that he was set on going to the lake for the holidays, and that go he would. Then the boss let him have his way, afraid to lose a man useful beyond the common, and of such experience in the bush."

Eutrope Gagnon was speaking with unusual ease, slowly, but without seeking words, as though his story had been shaped beforehand. Amid her overwhelming grief the thought flitted through Maria's heart:—"François wished to come here . . . to me," and a fugitive joy touched it as a swallow in flight ruffles the water with his wing.

"The shanty was not very far in the woods, only two days' journey from the Transcontinental which passes La Tuque. But as the luck was, something had happened to the line and the trains were not running. I heard all this through Johnny Niquette of St. Henri, who arrived from La Tuque two days ago."

"Yes."

"When François found that he could not take the train he burst into a laugh, and in that sort of a humour said that as it was a case of walking he would walk all the way—reaching the lake by following the rivers, first the Croche and then the Ouatchouan which falls in near Roberval."

"That is so," said Chapdelaine. "It can be done. I have gone that way."

"Not at this time of year, Mr. Chapdelaine, certainly not just at this time. Everyone there told François that it would be foolhardy to attempt such a trip in midwinter, about Christmas, with the cold as great as it was, some four feet of snow lying in the woods, and alone. But he only laughed and told them that he was used to the woods and that a little difficulty was not going to frighten him, because he was bound to get to the upper side of the lake for the holidays, and that where the Indians were able to cross he could make the crossing too. Only—you know it very well, Mr. Chapdelaine—when the Indians take that journey it is in company, and with their dogs. François set off alone, on snow-shoes, pulling his blankets and provisions on a toboggan."

No one had uttered a word to hasten or check the speaker. They listened as to him whose story's end stalks into view, before the eyes but darkly veiled, like a figure drawing near who hides his face.

"You will remember the weather a week before Christmas—the heavy snow that fell, and after it the nor'west gale. It happened that François was then in the great burnt lands, where the fine snow drives and drifts so terribly. In such a place the best of men have little chance when it is very cold and the storm lasts. And, if you recall it, the nor'wester was blowing for three days on end, stiff enough to flay you."

"Yes, and then?"

The narrative he had framed did not carry him further, or perhaps he could not bring himself to speak the final words, for it was some time before the low-voiced answer came:—"He went astray . . ."

Those who have passed their lives within the shadow of the Canadian forests know the meaning but too well. The daring youths to whom this evil fortune happens in the woods, who go astray—are lost—but seldom return. Sometimes a search-party finds their bodies in the spring, after the melting of the snows. In Quebec, and above all in the far regions of the north, the very word, *écarté*, has taken on a new and sinister import, from the peril overhanging him who loses his way, for a short day only, in that limitless forest.

"He went astray . . . The storm caught him in the burnt country and he halted for a day. So much we know, for the Indians found a shelter of fir branches he had made for himself, and they saw his tracks. He set out again because his provisions were low and he was in haste to reach the end of his journey, as I suppose; but the weather did not mend, snow was falling, the nor'west wind never eased, and it is likely he caught no glimpse of the sun to guide him, for the Indians said that his tracks turned off from the river Croche which he had been following and wandered away, straight to the north."

There was no further speech; neither from the two men who had listened with assenting motions of their heads while they followed every turn of Eutrope's grim story; nor from the mother whose hands were clasped upon her knees, as in a belated supplication; nor from Maria . . .

"When they heard this, men from Ouatchouan set forth after the weather was a little better. But all his footsteps were covered, and they returned saying that they had found no trace; that was three days ago . . . He is lost . . ."

The listeners stirred, and broke the stillness with a sigh; the tale was told, nor was there a word that anyone might speak. The fate of

François Paradis was as mournfully sure as though he were buried in the cemetery at St. Michel de Mistassini to the sound of chants, with the blessing of a priest.

Silence fell upon the house and all within it. Chapdelaine was leaning forward, elbows on his knees, his face working, mechanically striking one fist upon the other. At length he spoke:—"It shows we are but little children in the hand of the good God. François was one of the best men of these parts in the woods, and at finding his way; people who came here used to take him as guide, and always did he bring them back without mishap. And now he himself is lost. We are but little children. Some there be who think themselves pretty strong—able to get on without God's help in their houses and on their lands . . . but in the bush . . ." With solemn voice and slowly-moving head he repeated: "We are but little children."

"A good man he was," said Eutrope Gagnon, "in very truth a good man, strong and brave, with ill-will to none."

"Indeed that is true. I am not saying that the good God had cause to send him to his

[163]

death—him more than another. He was a
fine fellow, hard-working, and I loved him
well. But it shows you . . ."

"No one ever had a thing against him."
Eutrope's generous insistence carried him on.
"A man hard to match for work, afraid of
nothing and obliging withal. Everyone who
knew him was fond of him—you will not find
his like."

Raising his eyes to Maria he repeated with
emphasis:—"He was a good man, you will
not find his like."

"When we were at Mistassini," began
Madame Chapdelaine, "seven years ago,
he was only a lad, but very strong and
quick and as tall as he is now—I mean as he
was when he came here last summer. Always
good-natured too. No one could help liking
him."

They all looked straight before them in
speaking, and yet what they said seemed to
be for Maria alone, as if the dear secret of her
heart were open to them. But she spoke not,
nor moved, her eyes fixed upon the frosted
panes of the little window, impenetrable as
the wall.

Eutrope Gagnon did not linger. The Chapdelaines, left to themselves, were long without speech. At last the father said in a halting voice:—"François Paradis was almost alone in the world; now, as we all had an affection for him, we perhaps might have a mass or two said. What do you think, Laura?"

"Yes indeed. Three high masses with music, and when the boys return from the woods—in health, if such be the will of the good God—three more for the repose of his soul, poor lad! And every Sunday we shall say a prayer for him."

"He was like the rest of us," Chapdelaine continued, "not without fault, of course, but kindly and well-living. God and the Holy Virgin will have pity on him."

Again silence. Maria well knew it was for her they said these things—aware of her grief and seeking to assuage it; but she was not able to speak, either to praise the dead or utter her sorrow. A hand had fastened upon her throat, stifling her, as the narrative unfolded and the end loomed inevitable; and now this hand found its way into her breast and was crushing her heart. Presently she would know a yet more intolerable pain, but now she only felt the deadly grasp of those five fingers closed about her heart.

Other words were said, but they scarce reached her ear; then came the familiar evening stir of preparation for the night, the father's departure on a last visit to the stable and his swift return, face red with the cold, slamming the door hastily in a swirl of frosty vapour.

"Come, Maria." The mother called her very gently, and laid a hand upon her shoulder. She rose and went to kneel and pray with the others. Voice answered to voice for ten minutes, murmuring the sacred words in low monotone.

The usual prayer at an end, the mother whispered:—"Yet five Paters and five Aves for the souls of those who have suffered misfortune in the forest." And the voices again rose, this time more subdued, breaking sometimes to a sob.

When they were silent, and all had risen after the last sign of the cross, Maria went back to the window. The frost upon the panes made of them so many fretted squares

through which the eye could not penetrate,
shutting away the outside world; but Maria
saw them not, for the tears welled to her eyes
and blinded her. She stood there motionless,
with arms hanging piteously by her side, a
stricken figure of grief; then a sudden anguish
yet keener and more unbearable seized upon
her; blindly she opened the door and went out
upon the step.

The world that lay beyond the threshold,
sunk in moveless white repose, was of an im-
mense serenity; but when Maria passed from
the sheltering walls the cold smote her like
the hungry blade of a sword and the forest
leaped toward her in menace, its inscrutable
face concealing a hundred dreadful secrets
which called aloud to her in lamentable
voices. With a little moan she drew back, and
closing the door sat shivering beside the stove.
Numbness was yielding, sorrow taking on an
edge, and the hand that clutched her heart set
itself to devising new agonies, each one
subtler and more cruel than the last.

How he must have suffered, far off there
amid the snows! So thought she, as still her
own face remembered the sting of the bitter

air. Men threatened by this fate had told her that death coming in such a guise smote with gentle and painless hand—a hand that merely lulled to sleep; but she could not make herself believe it, and all the sufferings that François might have endured before giving up and falling to the white ground passed before her eyes.

No need for her to see the spot; too well she knew the winter terrors of the great forest, the snow heaped to the firs' lower branches, alders almost buried beneath it, birches and aspens naked as skeletons and shuddering in the icy wind, a sunless sky above the massed and gloomy spires of green. She sees François making his way through the close-set trees, limbs stiffened with the cold, his skin raw with that pitiless nor'wester, gnawed by hunger, stumbling with fatigue, his feet so weary that with no longer strength to lift them his snowshoes often catch the snow and throw him to his knees.

Doubtless when the storm abated he saw his error, knew that he was walking toward the barren northland, turned at once and took the right course—he so experienced, the

woods his home from boyhood. But his food
is nearly gone, the cold tortures him; with
lowered head and clenched teeth he fights the
implacable winter, calling to aid his every
reserve of strength and high courage. He
thinks of the road he must follow, the miles to
be overcome, measures his chances of life;
and fitful memories arise of a house, so warm
and snug, where all will greet him gladly; of
Maria who, knowing what he has dared for
her sake, will at length raise to him her
truthful eyes shining with love.

Perhaps he fell for the last time when succour was near, a few yards only from house or
shanty. Often so it happens. Cold and his
ministers of death flung themselves upon him
as their prey; they have stilled the strong
limbs forever, covered his open handsome face
with snow, closed the fearless eyes without
gentleness or pity, changed his living body
into a thing of ice . . . Maria has no more
tears that she may shed, but she shivers and
trembles as he must have trembled and shivered before he sank into merciful unconscious-
ness; horror and pity in her face, Maria draws
nearer the stove as though she might thus

bring nim warmth and shield his dear life
against the assassin.

"O Christ Jesus, who didst stretch forth
Thine arm to those in need, why didst Thou
not disperse the snows with those pale hands
of Thine? Holy Virgin, why didst Thou not
sustain him by Thy power when, for the last
time, his feet were stumbling? In all the legions of heaven why was there found no angel
to show him the way?"

But it is her grief that utters these re-
proaches, and the steadfast heart of Maria is
fearful of having sinned in yielding to it.
Another dread is soon to assail her. Perhaps
François Paradis was not able quite faithfully
to keep the promises he made to her. In the
shanty, among rough and careless men, may
he not have had moments of weakness;
blasphemed or taken the names of the saints
in vain, and thus have gone to his death with
sin upon his conscience, under the weight of
divine wrath.

Her parents had promised but a little ago
that masses should be said. How good they
were! Having guessed her secret how kindly
had they been silent! But she herself might

help with prayers the poor soul in torment. Her beads still lay upon the table; she takes them in her hands, and forthwith the words of the Ave mount to her lips:—"Hail Mary, full of grace . . ."

Did you doubt of her, O mother of the Galilean? Since that only eight days before she strove to reach your ear with her thousand prayers, and you but clothed yourself in divine impassivity while fate accomplished its purpose, think you that she questions your goodness or your power? It would indeed have been to misjudge her. As once she sought your aid for a man, so now she asks your pardon for a soul, in the same words, with the same humility and boundless faith.

"Blessed art Thou amongst women, and blessed is the fruit of Thy womb, Jesus."

But still she cowers by the great stove, and though the fire's heat strikes through her, she ceases not to shudder as she thinks of the frozen world about her, of François Paradis, who cannot be insentient, who must be so bitter cold in his bed of snow . . .

CHAPTER XI

THE INTERPRETER OF GOD

CHAPTER XI

THE INTERPRETER OF GOD

ONE evening in February Samuel Chapdelaine said to his daughter: "The roads are passable; if you wish it, Maria, we shall go to La Pipe on Sunday for the mass."

"Very well, father;" but she replied in a voice so dejected, almost indifferent, that her parents exchanged glances behind her back.

Country folk do not die for love, nor spend the rest of their days nursing a wound. They are too near to nature, and know too well the stern laws that rule their lives. Thus it is perhaps, that they are sparing of high-sounding words; choosing to say "liking" rather than "loving," "ennui" rather than "grief," that so the joys and sorrows of the heart may bear a fit proportion to those more anxious concerns of life which have to do with their daily toil, the yield of their lands, provision for the future.

Maria did not for a moment dream that life for her was over, or that the world must henceforward be a sad wilderness, because François Paradis would not return in the spring nor ever again. But her heart was aching, and while sorrow possessed it the future held no promise for her.

When Sunday arrived, father and daughter early began to make ready for the two hours' journey which would bring them to St. Henri de Taillon, and the church. Before half-past seven Charles Eugene was harnessed, and Maria, still wearing a heavy winter cloak, had carefully deposited in her purse the list of her mother's commissions. A few minutes later the sleigh-bells were tinkling, and the rest of the family grouped themselves at the little square window to watch the departure.

For the first hour the horse could not go beyond a walk, sinking knee-deep in snow; for only the Chapdelaines used this road, laid out and cleared by themselves, and not enough travelled to become smooth and hard. But when they reached the beaten highway Charles Eugene trotted along briskly.

They passed through Honfleur, a hamlet of eight scattered houses, and then re-entered the woods. After a time they came upon clearings, then houses appeared dotted along the road; little by little the dusky ranks of the forest retreated, and soon they were in the village with other sleighs before and following them, all going toward the church.

Since the beginning of the year Maria had gone three times to hear mass at St. Henri de Taillon, which the people of the country persist in calling La Pipe, as in the gallant days of the first settlers. For her, besides being an exercise of piety, this was almost the only distraction possible and her father sought to furnish it whenever he could do so, believing that the impressive rites of the church and a meeting with acquaintances in the village would help to banish her grief.

On this occasion when the mass was ended, instead of paying visits they went to the *curé's* house. It was already thronged with members of the congregation from remote farms, for the Canadian priest not only has the consciences of his flock in charge, but is their counsellor in all affairs, and the com-

[177]

poser of their disputes; the solitary individual
of different station to whom they can resort
for the solving of their difficulties.

The *curé* of St. Henri sent none away empty
who asked his advice; some he dealt with in a
few swift words amidst a general conversation
where he bore his cheerful part; others at
greater length in the privacy of an adjoining
room. When the turn of the Chapdelaines·
came he looked at his watch.

"We shall have dinner first. What say you,
my good friends? You must have found an
appetite on the road. As for myself, singing
mass makes me hungry beyond anything you
could believe."

He laughed heartily, more tickled than anyone at his own joke, and led his guests into
the dining-room. Another priest was there
from a neighbouring parish, and two or three
farmers. The meal was one long discussion
about husbandry, with a few amusing stories
and bits of harmless gossip thrown in; now
and then one of the farmers, suddenly remem-
bering where he was, would labour some pious
remark which the priests acknowledged with
a nod or an absent-minded "Yes! Yes!"

The dinner over at last, some of the guests departed after lighting their pipes. The *curé*, catching a glance from Chapdelaine, seemed to recall something; arising, he motioned to Maria, and went before her into the next room which served him both for visitors and as his office.

A small harmonium stood against the wall; on the other side was a table with agricultural journals, a Civil Code and a few books bound in black leather; on the walls hung a portrait of Pius X., an engraving of the Holy Family, the coloured broadside of a Quebec merchant with sleighs and threshing-machines side by side, and a number of official notices as to precautions against forest fires and epidemics amongst cattle.

Turning to Maria, the *curé* said kindly enough:—"So it appears that you are distressing yourself beyond what is reasonable and right?"

She looked at him humbly, not far from believing that the priest's supernatural power had divined her trouble without need of telling. He inclined his tall figure, and bent toward her his thin peasant face; for beneath

the robe was still the tiller of the soil: the
gaunt and yellow visage, the cautious eyes,
the huge bony shoulders. Even his hands—
hands wont to dispense the favours of Heaven
—were those of the husbandman, with
swollen veins beneath the dark skin. But
Maria saw in him only the priest, the *curé* of
the parish, appointed of God to interpret life
to her and show her the path of duty.

"Be seated there," he said, pointing to a
chair. She sat down somewhat like a school-
girl who is to have a scolding, somewhat like
a woman in a sorcerer's den who awaits in
mingled hope and dread the working of his
unearthly spells.

.   .   .   .

An hour later the sleigh was speeding over
the hard snow. Chapdelaine drowsed, and
the reins were slipping from his open hands.
Rousing himself and lifting his head, he sang
again in full-voiced fervour the hymn he was
singing as they left the village:—

> . . . Adorons-le dans le ciel.
> Adorons-le sur l'autel . . .

Then he fell silent, his chin dropping
slowly toward his breast, and the only

4

4

3

3

sound upon the road was the tinkle of sleigh-
bells.

Maria was thinking of the priest's words:
"If there was affection between you it is very
proper that you should know regret. But you
were not pledged to one another, because
neither you nor he had spoken to your parents; therefore it is not befitting or right that
you should sorrow thus, nor feel so deep a
grief for a young man who, after all is said,
was nothing to you . . ."

And again: "That masses should be sung,
that you should pray for him, such things are
useful and good, you could do no better.
Three high masses with music, and three more
when the boys return from the woods, as your
father has asked me, most assuredly these will
help him, and also you may be certain they
will delight him more than your lamentations,
since they will shorten by so much his time of
expiation. But to grieve like this, and to go
about casting gloom over the household is not
well, nor is it pleasing in the sight of God."

He did not appear in the guise of a com-
forter, nor of one who gives counsel in the
secret affairs of the heart, but rather as a man

of the law or a chemist who enunciates his bald formulas, invariable and unfailing.

'The duty of a girl like you—good-looking, healthy, active withal and a clever house-wife—is in the first place to help her old parents, and in good time to marry and bring up a Christian family of her own. You have no call to the religious life? No. Then you must give up torturing yourself in this fash-ion, because it is a sacrilegious thing and unseemly, seeing that the young man was nothing whatever to you. The good God knows what is best for us; we should neither rebel nor complain . . ."

In all this, but one phrase left Maria a little doubting, it was the priest's assurance that François Paradis, in the place where now he was, cared only for masses to repose his soul, and never at all for the deep and tender regrets lingering behind him. This she could not constrain herself to believe. Unable to think of him otherwise in death than in life, she felt it must bring him something of happiness and consolation that her sorrow was keeping alive their ineffectual love for a little space beyond death. Yet, since the priest had said it . . .

The road wound its way among the trees rising sombrely from the snow. Here and there a squirrel, alarmed by the swiftly passing sleigh and the tinkling bells, sprang upon a trunk and scrambled upward, clinging to the bark. From the gray sky a biting cold was falling and the wind stung the cheek, for this was February, with two long months of winter yet to come.

As Charles Eugene trotted along the beaten road, bearing the travellers to their lonely house, Maria, in obedience to the words of the *curé* at St. Henri, strove to drive away gloom and put mourning from her; as simple-mindedly as she would have fought the temptation of a dance, of a doubtful amusement or anything that was plainly wrong and hence forbidden.

They reached home as night was falling. The coming of evening was only a slow fading of the light, for, since morning, the heavens had been overcast, the sun obscured. A sadness rested upon the pallid earth; the firs and cypresses did not wear the aspect of living trees and the naked birches seemed to doubt of the springtime. Maria shivered as she left

[183]

the sleigh, and hardly noticed Chien, barking
and gambolling a welcome, or the children
who called to her from the door-step. The
world seemed strangely empty, for this
evening at least. Love was snatched away,
and they forbade remembrance. She went
swiftly into the house without looking about
her, conscious of a new dread and hatred for
the bleak land, the forest's eternal shade, the
snow and the cold,—for all those things she
had lived her life amongst, which now had
wounded her.

CHAPTER XII

LOVE BEARING GIFTS

CHAPTER XII

LOVE BEARING GIFTS

ARCH came, and one day Tit'Bé brought the news from Honfleur that there would be a large gathering in the evening at Ephrem Surprenant's to which everyone was invited.

But someone must stay to look after the house, and as Madame Chapdelaine had set her heart on this little diversion after being cooped up for all these months, it was Tit'Bé himself who was left at home. Honfleur, the nearest village to their house, was eight miles away; but what were eight miles over the snow and through the woods compared with the delight of hearing songs and stories, and of talk with people from afar?

A numerous company was assembled under the Surprenant roof: several of the villagers, the three Frenchmen who had bought his nephew Lorenzo's farm, and also, to the Chapdelaines' great surprise, Lorenzo himself, back once more from the States upon business that related to the sale and the settling of his father's affairs. He greeted Maria very warmly, and seated himself beside her.

The men lit their pipes; they chatted about the weather, the condition of the roads, the country news; but the conversation lagged, as though all were looking for it to take some unusual turn. Their glances sought Lorenzo and the three Frenchmen, expecting strange and marvellous tales of distant lands and unfamiliar manners from an assembly so far out of the common. The Frenchmen, only a few months in the country, apparently felt a like curiosity, for they listened, and spoke but little.

Samuel Chapdelaine, who was meeting them for the first time, deemed himself called upon to put them through a catechism in the ingenuous Canadian fashion.

"So you have come here to till the land. How do you like Canada?"

"It is a beautiful country, new and so vast . . . In the summer-time there are many flies, and the winters are trying; but I suppose that one gets used to these things in time."

[188]

The father it was who made reply, his sons only nodding their heads in assent with eyes glued to the floor. Their appearance alone would have served to distinguish them from the other dwellers in the village, but as they spoke the gap widened, and the words that fell from their lips had a foreign ring. There was none of the slowness of the Canadian speech, nor of that indefinable accent found in no corner of France, which is only a peasant blend of the different pronunciations of former emigrants. They used words and turns of phrase one never hears in Quebec, even in the towns, and which to these simple men seemed fastidious and wonderfully refined.

"Before coming to these parts were you farmers in your own country?"

"No."

"What trade then did you follow?"

The Frenchman hesitated a moment before replying; possibly thinking that what he was about to say would be novel, and hard for them to understand. "I was a tuner myself, a piano-tuner; my two sons here were clerks, Edmond in an office, Pierre in a shop."

Clerks—that was plain enough for anyone; but their minds were a little hazy as to the father's business.

However Ephrem Surprenant chimed in with:—"Piano-tuner; that was it, just so!" And his glance at Conrad Neron his neighbour was a trifle superior and challenging, as though intimating:—"You would not believe me, and maybe you don't know what it means, but now you see . . ."

"Piano-tuner," Samuel Chapdelaine echoed in turn, slowly grasping the meaning of the words. "And is that a good trade? Do you earn handsome wages? Not too handsome, eh! . . . At any rate you are well educated, you and your sons; you can read and write and cipher? And here am I, not able even to read!"

"Nor I!" struck in Ephrem Surprenant, and Conrad Neron and Egide Racicot added: "Nor I!" "Nor I!" in chorus, whereupon the whole of them broke out laughing.

A motion of the Frenchman's hand told them indulgently that they could very well dispense with these accomplishments; to himself of little enough use at the moment.

"You were not able to make a decent living out of your trades over there. That is so, is it not? And therefore you came here?"

The question was put simply, without thought of offence, for he was amazed that anyone should abandon callings that seemed so easy and so pleasant for this arduous life on the land.

Why indeed had they come? . . . A few months earlier they would have discovered a thousand reasons and clothed them in words straight from the heart: weariness of the foot-way and the pavement, of the town's sullied air; revolt against the prospect of lifelong slavery; some chance stirring word of an irresponsible speaker preaching the gospel of vigour and enterprise, of a free and healthy life upon a fruitful soil. But a few months ago they could have found glowing sentences to tell it all . . . Now their best was a sorry effort to evade the question, as they groped for any of the illusions that remained to them.

"People are not always happy in the cities," said the father. "Everything is dear, and one is confined."

In their narrow Parisian lodging it had seemed so wonderful a thing to them, the notion that in Canada they would spend their days out of doors, breathing the taintless air of a new country, close beside the mighty forest. The black-flies they had not foreseen, nor comprehended the depth of the winter's cold; the countless ill turns of a land that has no pity were undivined.

"Did you picture it to yourselves as you have found it," Chapdelaine persisted, "the country here, the life?"

"Not exactly," replied the Frenchman in a low voice. "No, not exactly . . ." And a shadow crossed his face which brought from Ephrem Surprenant:—"It is rough here, rough and hard!"

Their heads assented, and their eyes fell: three narrow-shouldered men, their faces with the pallor of the town still upon them after six months on the land; three men whom a fancy had torn from counter, office, piano-stool—from the only lives for which they were bred. For it is not the peasant alone who suffers by uprooting from his native soil. They were seeing their mistake, and knew they were too unlike in grain to copy those about them; lacking the strength, the rude health, the toughened fibre, that training for every task which fits the Canadian to be farmer, woodsman or carpenter, according to season and need.

The father was dreamily shaking his head, lost in thought; one of the sons, elbows on knees, gazed wonderingly at the palms of his delicate hands, calloused by the rough work of the fields. All three seemed to be turning over and over in their minds the melancholy balance-sheet of a failure. Those about them were thinking:—"Lorenzo sold his place for more than it was worth; they have but little money left and are in hard case; men like these are not built for living on the land."

Madame Chapdelaine, partly in pity and partly for the honour of farming, let fall a few encouraging words:—"It is something of a struggle at the beginning—if you are not used to it; but when your land is in better order you will see that life becomes easier."

"It is a queer thing," said Conrad Neron, "how every man finds it equally hard to rest content. Here are three who left their homes and came this long way to settle and farm, and here am I always saying to myself that nothing would be so pleasant as to sit quietly in an office all the day, a pen behind my ear, sheltered from cold wind and hot sun."

"Everyone to his own notion," declared Lorenzo Surprenant, with unbiassed mind.

"And your notion is not to stick in Honfleur sweating over the stumps," added Racicot with a loud laugh.

"You are quite right there, and I make no bones about it; that sort of thing would never have suited me. These men here bought my land—a good farm, and no one can gainsay it. They wanted to buy a farm and I sold them mine. But as for myself, I am well enough where I am, and have no wish to return."

Madame Chapdelaine shook her head. "There is no better life than the life of a farmer who has good health and owes no debts. He is a free man, has no boss, owns his beasts, works for his own profit . . . The finest life there is!"

"I hear them all say that," Lorenzo retorted, "one is free, his own master. And you seem to pity those who work in factories be-

cause they have a boss, and must do as they
are told. Free—on the land—come now!"
He spoke defiantly, with more and more
animation.

"There is no man in the world less free
than a farmer . . . When you tell of those
who have succeeded, who are well provided
with everything needful on a farm, who have
had better luck than others, you say:—'Ah,
what a fine life they lead! They are comfortably off, own good cattle.' That is not how to
put it. The truth is that their cattle own
them. In all the world there is no 'boss' who
behaves as stupidly as the beasts you favour.
Pretty nearly every day they give you trouble
or do you some mischief. Now it is a skittish
horse that runs away or lashes out with his
heels; then it is a cow, however good-tem-
pered, that won't keep still to be milked and
tramples on your toes when the flies annoy her.
And even if by good fortune they don't harm
you, they are forever finding a way to destroy
your comfort and to vex you . . ."

"I know how it is; I was brought up on a
farm. And you, most of you farmers, know
how it is too. All the morning you have

worked hard, and go to your house for dinner and a little rest. Then, before you are well seated at table, a child is yelling:—'The cows are over the fence;' or 'The sheep are in the crop,' and everyone jumps up and runs, thinking of the oats or the barley it has been such a trouble to raise, that these miserable fools are ruining. The men dash about brandishing sticks till they are out of breath; the women stand screaming in the farm-yard. And when you have managed to drive the cows or the sheep into their paddock and put up the rails, you get back to the house nicely 'rested' to find the pea-soup cold and full of flies, the pork under the table gnawed by dogs and cats, and you eat what you can lay your hands on, watching for the next trick the wretched animals are getting ready to play on you."

"You are their slaves; that's what you are. You tend them, you clean them, you gather up their dung as the poor do the rich man's crumbs. It is you who must keep them alive by hard work, because the earth is miserly and the summer so short. That is the way of it, and there is no help, as you cannot get on without them; but for cattle there would be no living on the land. But even if you could . . . even if you could . . . still would you have other masters: the summer, beginning too late and ending too soon; the winter, eating up seven long months of the year and bringing in nothing; drought and rain which always come just at the wrong moment . . ."

"In the towns these things do not matter; but here you have no defence against them and they do you hurt; and I have not taken into account the extreme cold, the badness of the roads, the loneliness of being far away from everything, with no amusements. Life is one kind of hardship on top of another from beginning to end. It is often said that only those make a real success who are born and brought up on the land, and of course that is true; as for the people in the cities, small danger that they would ever be foolish enough to put up with such a way of living."

He spoke with heat and volubly—a man of the town who talks every day with his equals, reads the papers, hears public speakers. The listeners, of a race easily moved by words, were carried away by his plaints and criticisms; the very real harshness of their lives was presented in such a new and startling light as to surprise even themselves.

However Madame Chapdelaine again shook her head. "Do not say such things as that; there is no happier life in the world than the life of a farmer who owns good land."

"Not in these parts, Madame Chapdelaine. You are too far north; the summer is too short; the grain is hardly up before the frosts come.   Each time that I return from the States, and see the tiny wooden houses lost in this wilderness—so far from one another that they seem frightened at being alone—and the woods hemming you in on every side . . . By Heaven! I lose heart for you, I who live here no longer, and I ask myself how it comes about that all you folk did not long ago seek a kinder climate where you would find everything that makes for comfort, where you could go out for a walk in the winter-time without being in fear of death . . ."

Without being in fear of death! Maria shuddered as the thought swiftly awoke of those dark secrets hidden beneath the everlasting green and white of the forest. Lorenzo

Surprenant was right in what he had been saying; it was a pitiless ungentle land. The menace lurking just outside the door—the cold—the shrouding snows—the blank solitude—forced a sudden entrance and crowded about the stove, an evil swarm sneering presages of ill or hovering in a yet more dreadful silence:—"Do you remember, my sister, the men, brave and well-beloved, whom we have slain and hidden in the woods? Their souls have known how to escape us; but their bodies, their bodies, their bodies, none shall ever snatch them from our hands . . ."

The voice of the wind at the corners of the house was loud with hollow laughter, and to Maria it seemed that all gathered within the wooden walls huddled and spoke low, like men whose lives are under a threat and who go in dread.

A burden of sadness was upon the rest of the evening, at least for her. Racicot told stories of the chase: of trapped bears struggling and growling so fiercely at the sight of the trapper that he loses courage and falls a-trembling; and then giving up suddenly when the hunters come in force and the deadly guns are aimed—giving up, covering their heads with their paws and whimpering with groans and outcries almost human, very heart-rending and pitiful.

After these tales came others of ghosts and apparitions; of blood-curdling visitations or solemn warnings to men who had blasphemed or spoken ill of the priests. Then, as no one could be persuaded to sing, they played at cards and the conversation dropped to more commonplace themes. The only memory that Maria carried away of the later talk, as the sleigh bore them homeward through the midnight woods, was of Lorenzo Surprenant extolling the United States and the magnificence of its great cities, the easy and pleasant life, the never-ending spectacle of the fine straight streets flooded with light at evening.

Before she departed Lorenzo said in quiet tones, almost in her ear:—"To-morrow is Sunday; I shall be over to see you in the afternoon."

A few short hours of night, a morning of sunlight on the snow, and again he is by her side renewing his tale of wonders, his inter-

rupted plea. For it was to her he had been
speaking the evening before; Maria knew it
well. The scorn he showed for a country
life, his praises of the town, these were but
a preface to the allurements he was about
to offer in all their varied forms, as one shows
the pictures in a book, turning page by page.

"Maria," he began, "you have not the
faintest idea! As yet, the most wonderful
things you ever saw were the shops in Roberval, a high mass, an evening entertainment
at the convent with acting. City people
would laugh to think of it! You simply cannot imagine . . . Just to stroll through the
big streets in the evening—not on little
plank-walks like those of Roberval, but on
fine broad asphalt pavements as level as a
table—just that and no more, what with the
lights, the electric cars coming and going
continually, the shops and the crowds, you
would find enough there to amaze you for
weeks together. And then all the amusements one has: theatres, circusses, illustrated
papers, and places everywhere that you can
go into for a nickel—five cents—and pass
two hours laughing and crying. To think,

Maria, you do not even know what the moving pictures are!"

He stopped for a little, reviewing in his mind the marvels of the cinematograph, asking himself whether he could hope to describe convincingly the fare it provided:— those thrilling stories of young girls, deserted or astray, which crowd the screen with twelve minutes of heart-rending misery and three of amends and heavenly reward in surroundings of incredible luxury;—the frenzied galloping of cowboys in pursuit of Indian ravishers; the tremendous fusillade; the rescue at the last conceivable second by soldiers arriving in a whirlwind, waving triumphantly the star-spangled banner . . . after pausing in doubt he shook his head, conscious that he had no words to paint such glories.

They walked on snow-shoes side by side over the snow, through the burnt lands that lie on the Peribonka's high bank above the fall. Lorenzo had used no wile to secure Maria's company, he simply invited her before them all, and now he told of his love in the same straightforward practical way.

"The first day I saw you, Maria, the very first day . . . that is only the truth! For a long time I had not been back in this country, and I was thinking what a miserable place it was to live in, that the men were a lot of simpletons who had never seen anything and the girls not nearly so quick and clever as they are in the States . . . And then, the moment I set eyes on you, there was I saying to myself that I was the simpleton, for neither at Lowell nor Boston had I ever met a girl like yourself. When I returned I used to be thinking a dozen times a day that some wretched farmer would make love to you and carry you off, and every time my heart sank. It was on your account that I came back, Maria, came up here from near Boston, three days' journey! The business I had, I could have done it all by letter; it was you I wished to see, to tell you what was in my heart to say and to hear the answer you would give me."

Wherever the snow was clear for a few yards, free of dead trees and stumps, and he could lift his eyes without fear of stumbling, they were fixed upon Maria; between the woollen cap and the long woollen jersey curving to her vigorous form he saw the outline of her face, downward turned, expressing only gentleness and patience. Every glance gave fresh reason for his love but brought him no hint of a response.

"This . . . this is no place for you, Maria. The country is too rough, the work too hard; barely earning one's bread is killing toil. In a factory over there, clever and strong as you are, soon you would be in the way of making nearly as much as I do; but no need of that if you were my wife. I earn enough for both of us, and we should have every comfort: good clothes to wear, a pretty flat in a brick house with gas and hot water, and all sorts of contrivances you never heard of to save you labour and worry every moment of the day. And don't let the idea enter your head that all the people are English. I know many Canadian families who work as I do or even keep shops. And there is a splendid church with a Canadian priest as *curé*—Mr. Tremblay from St. Hyacinthe. You would never be lonesome . . ."

Pausing again he surveyed the white plain with its ragged crop of brown stumps, the bleak plateau dropping a little farther in a long slope to the levels of the frozen river; meanwhile ransacking his mind for some final persuasive word.

"I hardly know what to say . . . You have always lived here and it is not possible for you to guess what life is elsewhere, nor would I be able to make you understand were I to talk forever. But I love you, Maria, I earn a good wage and I never touch a drop. If you will marry me as I ask I will take you off to a country that will open your eyes with astonishment—a fine country, not a bit like this, where we can live in a decent way and be happy for the rest of our days."

Maria still was silent, and yet the sentences of Lorenzo Surprenant beat upon her heart as succeeding waves roll against the shore. It was not his avowals of love, honest and sincere though they were, but the lures he used which tempted her. Only of cheap pleasures had he spoken, of trivial things ministering to comfort or vanity, but of these alone was she able to conjure up a definite idea. All else—the distant glamour of the city, of a life new and incomprehensible to her, full in the centre of the bustling world and no longer at its very confines— enticed her but the more in its shimmering remoteness with the mystery of a great light that shines from afar.

Whatsoever there may be of wonder and exhilaration in the sight and touch of the crowd; the rich harvests of mind and sense for which the city dweller has bartered his rough heritage of pride in the soil, Maria was dimly conscious of as part of this other life in a new world, this glorious re-birth for which she was already yearning. But above all else the desire was strong upon her now to flee away, to escape.

The wind from the east was driving before it a host of melancholy snow-laden clouds. Threateningly they swept over white ground and sullen wood, and the earth seemed awaiting another fold of its winding-sheet; cypress, spruce and fir, close side by side and motionless, were passive in their attitude of uncomplaining endurance. The stumps above the snow were like floating wreckage on a dreary

[206]

sea. In all the landscape there was naught
that spoke of a spring to come—of warmth
and growth; rather did it seem a shard of
some disinherited planet under the eternal
rule of deadly cold.

All of her life had Maria known this cold,
this snow, the land's death-like sleep, these
austere and frowning woods; now was she
coming to view them with fear and hate. A
paradise surely must it be, this country to
the south where March is no longer winter
and in April the leaves are green! At midwinter one takes to the road without snow-
shoes, unclad in furs, beyond sight of the
cruel forest. And the cities . . . the pavements . . .

Questions framed themselves upon her
lips. She would know if lofty houses and
shops stood unbrokenly on both sides of the
streets, as she had been told; if the electric
cars ran all the year round; if the living was
very dear . . . And the answers to her
questions would have satisfied but a little of
this eager curiosity, would scarcely have
disturbed the enchanting vagueness of her
illusion.

She was silent, however, dreading to speak any word that might seem like the foreshadowing of a promise. Though Lorenzo gazed at her long as they walked together across the snow, he was able to guess nothing of what was passing in her heart.

"You will not have me, Maria? You have no liking for me, or is it, perhaps, that you cannot make up your mind?" As still she gave no reply he clung to this idea, fearing that she might hastily refuse him.

"No need whatever that you should say 'Yes' at once. You have not known me very long . . . But think of what I have said to you. I will come back, Maria. It is a long journey and costly, but I will come. And if only you give thought to it, you will see there is no young fellow here who could give you such a future as I can; because if you marry me we shall live like human beings, and not have to kill ourselves tending cattle and grubbing in the earth in this out-of-the-way corner of the world."

They returned to the house. Lorenzo gossiped a little about his journey to the States, where the springtime would have arrived before him, of the plentiful and well-paid work to which his good clothes and prosperous air bore witness. Then he bade them adieu, and Maria, whose eyes had carefully been avoiding his, seated herself by the window, and watched the night and the snow falling together as she pondered in the deep unrest of her spirit.

CHAPTER XIII

LOVE BEARING CHAINS

CHAPTER XIII

LOVE BEARING CHAINS

NO one asked Maria any questions that evening, or on the following evenings; but some member of the family must have told Eutrope Gagnon of Lorenzo Surprenant's visit and his evident intentions, for the next Sunday after dinner came Eutrope in turn, and Maria heard another suitor declare his love.

François had come in the full tide of summer, from the land of mystery at the headwaters of the rivers; the memory of his artless words brought back the dazzling sunshine, the ripened blueberries and the last blossoms of the laurel fading in the undergrowth; after him appeared Lorenzo Surprenant offering other gifts,—visions of beautiful distant cities, of a life abounding in unknown wonders. When Eutrope spoke, it was in a shamefaced halting way, as though he foresaw defeat, knowing full well that he bore little in his hands wherewith to tempt her.

Boldly enough he asked Maria to walk with him, but when they were dressed and outside the door, they saw that snow was falling. Maria stood dubiously on the step, a hand on the latch as though she would return; and Eutrope, unwilling to lose his chance, began forthwith to speak—hastening as though doubtful that he would be able to say all that was in his mind.

"You know very well, Maria, how I feel toward you. I said nothing before as my farm was not so forward that we could live there comfortably, and moreover I guessed that you liked François Paradis better than me. But as François is no longer here, and this young fellow from the States is courting you, I said to myself that I, too, might try my fortune . . ."

The snow was coming now in serried flakes, fluttering whitely for an instant against the darkly-encircling forest, on the way to join that other snow with which five months of winter had burdened the earth.

"It is true enough that I am not rich; but I have two lots of my own, paid for out and out, and you know the soil is good. I shall work on

it all spring, take the stumps out of the large
field below the ridge of rock, put up some
fences, and by May there will be a fine big
field ready for seeding. I shall sow a hundred
and thirty bushels, Maria,—a hundred and
thirty bushels of wheat, barley and oats, without reckoning an acre of mixed grain for the
cattle. All the seed, the best seed-grain, I am
going to buy at Roberval, settling for it on the
spot . . . I have the money put aside; I shall
pay cash, without running into debt to a soul,
and if only we have an average season there
will be a fine crop to harvest. Just think of it,
Maria, a hundred and thirty bushels of good
seed in first-rate land! And in the summer
before the hay-making, and then again before
the harvest, will be the best chance for build-
ing a nice tight warm little house, all of tamarack. I have the wood ready, cut and piled
behind my barn; my brother will help me,
perhaps Esdras and Da'Bé as well, when they
get home. Next winter I shall go to the
shanties, taking a horse with me, and in the
spring I shall bring back not less than two
hundred dollars in my pocket. Then, should

you be willing to wait so long for me, would be
the time . . ."

Maria was leaning against the door, a hand
still upon the latch, her eyes turned away.
Eutrope Gagnon had just the more to
offer her: after a year of waiting that she
should become his wife, and live as now she
was doing in another wooden house on another half-cleared farm . . . Should do the
household work and the cooking, milk the
cows, clean the stable when her man was
away—labour in the fields perhaps, since she
was strong and there would be but two of
them . . . Should spend her evenings at the
spinning-wheel or in patching old clothes
. . . Now and then in summer resting for
half an hour, seated on the door-step, looking
across their scant fields girt by the measure-
less frowning woods; or in winter thawing
a little patch with her breath on the window-
pane, dulled with frost, to watch the snow falling on the wintry earth and the forest . . .
The forest . . . Always the inscrutable,
inimical forest, with a host of dark things hiding there—closed round them with a savage
grip that must be loosened little by little, year

by year; a few acres won each spring and autumn as the years pass, throughout all the long days of a dull harsh life . . . No, that she could not face . . .

"I know well enough that we shall have to work hard at first," Eutrope went on, "but you have courage, Maria, and are well used to labour, as I am. I have always worked hard; no one can say that I was ever lazy, and if only you will marry me it will be my joy to toil like an ox all the day long to make a thriving place of it, so that we shall be in comfort before old age comes upon us. I do not touch drink, Maria, and truly I love you . . ."

His voice quivered, and he put out his hand toward the latch to take hers, or perhaps to hinder her from opening the door and leaving him without his answer.

"My affection for you . . . of that I am not able to speak . . ."

Never a word did she utter in reply. Once more a young man was telling his love, was placing in her hands all he had to give; and once more she could but hearken in mute embarrassment, only saved from awkwardness by her immobility and silence. Town-bred girls had thought her stupid, when she was but honest and truthful; very close to nature which takes no account of words. In other days when life was simpler than now it is, when young men paid their court—masterfully and yet half bashfully—to some deep-bosomed girl in the ripe fullness of womanhood who had not heard nature's imperious command, she must have listened thus, in silence; less attentive to their pleading than to the inner voice, guarding herself by distance against too ardent a wooing, whilst she awaited . . . The three lovers of Maria Chapdelaine were not drawn to her by any charm of gracious speech, but by her sheer comeliness, and the transparent honest heart dwelling in her bosom; when they spoke to her of love she was true to herself, steadfast and serene, saying no word where none was needful to be said, and for this they loved her only the more.

"This young fellow from the States was ready with fine speeches, but you must not be carried away by them . . ." He caught a hint of dissent and changed his tone.

"Of course you are quite free to choose, and I have not a word to say against him. But you would be happier here, Maria, amongst people like yourself."

Through the falling snow Maria gazed at the rude structure of planks, between stable and barn, which her father and brother had thrown together five years before; unsightly and squalid enough it appeared, now that her fancy had begun to conjure up the stately buildings of the town. Close and ill-smelling, the floor littered with manure and foul straw, the pump in one corner that was so hard to work and set the teeth on edge with its griding; the weather-beaten outside, buffeted by wind and never-ending snow—sign and symbol of what awaited her were she to marry one like Eutrope Gagnon, and accept as her lot a lifetime of rude toil in this sad and desolate land . . . She shook her head.

"I cannot answer, Eutrope, either yes or no; not just now. I have given no promise. You must wait."

It was more than she had said to Lorenzo Surprenant, and yet Lorenzo had gone away with hope in his heart, while Eutrope felt that

he had made his throw and lost. Departing
alone, the snow soon hid him. She entered
the house.

.   .   .   .

March dragged through its melancholy
days; cold winds drove the gray clouds back
and forth across the sky, and swept the snow
hither and thither; one must needs consult
the calendar of the Roberval grain merchant
to get an inkling that spring was drawing
near.

Succeeding days were to Maria like those
that had gone before, each one bringing its
familiar duties and the same routine; but the
evenings were different, and were filled with
pathetic strivings to think. Beyond doubt her
parents had guessed the truth; but they were
unwilling to force her reserve with their advice, nor did she seek it. She knew that it
rested with her alone to make a choice, to
settle the future course of her life, and she felt
like a child at school, standing on a platform
before watchful eyes, bidden to find by herself
the answer to some knotty question.

And this was her problem: when a girl is
grown to womanhood, when she is good-look-

ing, healthy and strong, clever in all that per-
tains to the household and the farm, young
men come and ask her to marry, and she must
say "Yes" to this one and "No" to another.

If only François Paradis had not vanished
forever in the great lonely woods, all were
then so plain. No need to ask herself what
she ought to do; she would have gone straight
to him, guided by a wise instinct that she
might not gainsay, sure of doing what was
right as a child that obeys a command. But
François was gone; neither in the promised
springtime nor ever again to return, and the
curé of St. Henri forbade regrets that would
prolong the awaiting.

Ah, dear God! How happy had been the
early days of this awaiting! As week followed
week something quickened in her heart and
shot upward, like a rich and beauteous sheaf
whose opening ears bend low under their
weight. Happiness beyond any dream came
dancing to her . . . No, it was stronger and
keener yet, this joy of hers. It had been a
great light shining in the twilight of a lonely
land, a beacon toward which one journeys,

forgetful of the tears that were about to flow, saying with glad defiance: "I knew it well— knew that somewhere on the earth was such a thing as this . . ." It was over. Yes, the gleam was gone. Henceforth must she forget that once it had shone upon her path, and grope through the dark with faltering steps.

Chapdelaine and Tit'Bé were smoking in silence by the stove; the mother knitted stockings; Chien, stretched out with his head between his paws, blinked sleepily in enjoyment of the good warmth. Telesphore had dozed off with the catechism open on his knees, and the little Alma Rose, not yet in bed, was hovering in doubt between the wish to draw attention to her brother's indolence, and a sense of shame at thus betraying him.

Maria looked down again, took her work in hand, and her simple mind pursued a little further its puzzling train of thought. When a girl does not feel, or feels no longer, that deep mysterious impulse toward a man singled out from all the rest of the world, what is left to guide her? For what things should she seek in her marriage? For a satisfying life, surely; to make a happy home for herself . . .

Her parents would like her to marry Eutrope Gagnon—that she felt—because she would live near them, and again because this life upon the land was the only one they knew, and they naturally thought it better than any other. Eutrope was a fine fellow, hard-working and of kindly disposition, and he loved her; but Lorenzo Surprenant also loved her; he, likewise, was steady and a good worker; he was a Canadian at heart, not less than those amongst whom she lived; he went to church . . . And he offered as his splendid gift a world dazzling to the eye, all the wonders of the city. He would rescue her from this oppression of frozen earth and gloomy forest.

She could not as yet resolve to say to herself: "I will marry Lorenzo Surprenant," but her heart had made its choice. The cruel north-west wind that heaped the snow above François Paradis at the foot of some desolate cypress bore also to her on its wings the frown and the harshness of the country wherein she dwelt, and filled her with hate of the northern winter, the cold, the whitened ground and the loneliness, of that boundless forest unheedful

of the destinies of men where every melancholy tree is fit to stand in a home of the dead.
Love—all-compelling love—for a brief space
had dwelt within her heart . . . Mighty
flame, scorching and bright, quenched now,
and never to revive. It left her spirit empty
and yearning; she was fain to seek forgetfulness and cure in that life afar, among the
myriad paler lights of the city.

CHAPTER XIV

INTO THE DEEP SILENCE

CHAPTER XIV

INTO THE DEEP SILENCE

T HERE came an evening in April when Madame Chapdelaine would not take her place at the supper table with the others.

"There are pains through my body and I have no appetite," she said, "I must have strained myself to-day lifting a bag of flour when I was making bread. Now something catches me in the back, and I am not hungry."

No one answered her. Those living sheltered lives take quick alarm when the mechanism of one of their number goes wrong, but people who wrestle with the earth for a living feel little surprise if their labours are too much for them now and then, and the body gives way in some fibre.

While father and children supped, Madame Chapdelaine sat very still in her chair beside the stove. She drew her breath hard, and her broad face was working.

[227]

"I am going to bed," she said presently. "A good night's sleep, and to-morrow morning I shall be all right again; have no doubt of that. You will see to the baking, Maria."

And indeed in the morning she was up at her usual hour, but when she had made the batter for the pancakes pain overcame her, and she had to lie down again. She stood for a minute beside the bed, with both hands pressed against her back, and made certain that the daily tasks would be attended to.

"You will give the men their food, Maria, and your father will lend you a hand at milking the cows if you wish it. I am not good for anything this morning."

"It will be all right, mother; it will be all right. Take it quietly; we shall have no trouble."

For two days she kept her bed, with a watchful eye over everything, directing all the household affairs.

"Don't be in the least anxious," her husband urged again and again. "There is hardly anything to be done in the house beyond the cooking, and Maria is quite fit to look after that—everything else too, by

[228]

thunder! She is not a little child any longer, and is as capable as yourself. Lie there quietly, without stirring; and be easy in your mind, instead of tossing about all the time under the blankets and making yourself worse."

On the third day she gave up thinking about the cares of the house and began to bemoan herself.

"Oh my God!" she wailed. "I have pains all over my body, and my head is burning. I think that I am going to die."

Her husband tried to cheer her with his clumsy pleasantries. "You are going to die when the good God wills it, and according to my way of thinking that will not be for a while yet. What would He be doing with you? Heaven is all cluttered with old women, and down here we have only the one, and she is able to make herself a bit useful, every now and then . . ." But he was beginning to feel anxious, and took counsel with his daughter.

"I could put the horse in and go as far as La Pipe," he suggested. "It may be that they have some medicine for this sickness at the store; or I might talk things over with the *curé*, and he would tell me what to do."

Before they had made up their minds night had fallen, and Tit'Bé, who had been at Eutrope Gagnon's helping him to saw his firewood, came back bringing Eutrope along with him.

"Eutrope has a remedy," said he. They all gathered round Eutrope, who took a little tin box from his pocket and opened it deliberately.

"This is what I have," he announced rather dubiously. "They are little pills. When my brother was bad with his kidneys three years ago he saw an advertisement in a paper about these pills, and it said they were the proper thing, so he sent the money for a box, and he declares it is a good medicine. Of course his trouble did not leave him at once, but he says that this did him good. It comes from the States . . ."

Without word said they looked at the little gray pills rolling about on the bottom of the box . . . A remedy compounded by some man in a distant land famed for his wisdom . . . And they felt the awe of the savage for his broth of herbs simmered on a night of the full moon beneath the medicine-man's incantations.

Maria asked doubtfully: "Is it certain that her trouble has only to do with the kidneys?"

"I thought it was just that, from what Tit'Bé told me."

A motion of Chapdelaine's hand eked out his words:—"She strained herself lifting a bag of flour, as she says; and now she has pains everywhere. How can we tell . . ."

"The newspaper that spoke of this medicine," Eutrope Gagnon went on, "put it that whenever a person falls sick and is in pain it is always the kidneys; and for trouble in the kidneys these pills here are first-rate. That is what the paper said, and my brother as well."

"Even if they are not for this very sickness," said Tit'Bé deferentially, "they are a remedy all the same."

"She suffers, that is one thing certain; we cannot let her go on like this."

They drew near the bed where the sick woman was moaning and breathing heavily, attempting from time to time to make slight

[231]

movements which were followed by sharper outcries.

"Eutrope has brought you a cure, Laura."

"I have no faith in your cures," she groaned out. But yet she was ready to look at the little gray pills ever running round in the tin box as if they were alive.

"My brother took some of these three years ago when he had the kidney trouble so badly that he was hardly able to work at all, and he says that they cured him. It is a fine remedy, Madame Chapdelaine, there is not a question of it!" His former doubts had vanished in speech and he felt wholly confident. "This is going to cure you, Madame Chapdelaine, as surely as the good God is above us. It is a medicine of the very first class; my brother had it sent expressly from the States. You may be sure that you would never find a medicine like this in the store at La Pipe."

"It cannot make her worse?" Maria asked, some doubt lingering. "It is not a poison, or anything of that sort?"

With one voice, in an indignant tone, the three men protested: "Do harm? Tiny pills no bigger than that!"

[232]

"My brother took nearly a box of them, and according to his account it was only good they did him."

When Eutrope departed he left the box of pills; the sick woman had not yet agreed to try them, but her objections grew weaker at their urging. In the middle of the night she took a couple, and two more in the morning, and as the hours passed they all waited in confidence for the virtue of the medicine to declare itself. But toward midday they had to bow to the facts: she was no easier and did not cease her moaning. By evening the box was empty, and at the falling of night her groans were filling the household with anguished distress, all the keener as they had no medicine now in which to place their trust.

Maria was up several times in the night, aroused by her mother's more piercing cries; she always found her lying motionless on her side, and this position seemed to increase the suffering and the stiffness, so that her groans were pitiful to hear.

"What ails you, mother? Are you not feeling any better?"

"Ah God, how I suffer! How I do suffer! I cannot stir myself, not the least bit, and even so the pain is as bad as ever. Give me some cold water, Maria; I have the most terrible thirst."

Several times Maria gave her mother water, but at last she became afraid. "Maybe it is not good for you to drink so much. Try to bear the thirst for a little."

"But I cannot bear it, I tell you—the thirst and the pain all through my body, and my head that burns like fire . . . My God! It is certain that I am to die."

A little before daylight they both fell asleep; but soon Maria was awakened by her father who laid his hand upon her shoulder and whispered:—"I am going to harness the horse to go to Mistook for the doctor, and on the way through La Pipe I shall also speak to the *curé*. It is heart-breaking to hear her moan like this."

Her eyes open in the ghostly dawn, Maria gave ear to the sounds of his departure: the banging of the stable door against the wall; the horse's hoofs thudding on the wood of the alley; muffled commands to Charles Eugene:

"Hold up, there!   Back . . . Back up!
Whoa!" Then the tinkle of the sleigh-bells.
In the silence that followed, the sick woman
groaned two or three times in her sleep; Maria
watched the wan light stealing into the house
and thought of her father's journey, trying
to reckon up the distances he must travel.

From their house to Honfleur, eight miles;
from Honfleur to La Pipe, six. There her
father would speak with the *curé*, and then
pursue his way to Mistook. She corrected
herself, and for the ancient Indian name that
the people of the country use, gave it the
official one bestowed in baptism by the
church—St. Cœur de Marie. From La Pipe
to St. Cœur de Marie, eight miles . . .
Eight and six and then eight. Growing confused, she said to herself:—"Anyway it is far,
and the roads will be heavy."

Again she felt affrighted at their loneliness,
which once hardly gave her a thought. All
was well enough when people were in health
and merry, and one had no need of help; but
with trouble or sickness the woods around
seemed to shut them cruelly away from all
succour—the woods where horses sink to the

chest in snow, where storms smother one in
mid-April.

The mother strove to turn in her sleep,
waked with a cry of anguish, and the continual moaning began anew. Maria rose and
sat by the bed, thinking of the long day just
beginning in which she would have neither
help nor counsel.

All the dragging hours were burdened with
lamentable sound; the groaning from the bed
where the sick woman lay never ceased, and
haunted the narrow wooden dwelling. Now
and then some household noise broke in upon
it: the clashing of plates, the clang of the
opened stove door, the sound of feet on the
planking, Tit'Bé stealing into the house,
clumsy and anxious, to ask for news.

"Is she no better?"

Maria answered by a movement of the
head. They both stood gazing for a time at
the motionless figure under the woollen blankets, giving ear to the sounds of distress; then
Tit'Bé departed to his small outdoor duties.
When Maria had put the house in order she
took up her patient watching, and the sick

woman's agonizing wails seemed to reproach her.

From hour to hour she kept reckoning the times and the distances. "My father should not be far from St. Cœur de Marie . . . If the doctor is there they will rest the horse for a couple of hours and come back together. But the roads must be very bad; at this time, in the spring, they are sometimes hardly passable."

And then a little later:—"They should have left; perhaps in going through La Pipe they will stop to speak to the *curé;* perhaps again he may have started as soon as he heard, without waiting for them. In that case he might be here at any moment."

But the fall of night brought no one, and it was only about seven o'clock that the sound of sleigh-bells was heard, and her father and the doctor arrived. The latter came into the house alone, put his bag on the table and began to pull off his overcoat, grumbling all the while.

"With the roads in this condition," said he, "it is no small affair to get about and visit the sick. And as for you folk, you seem to have hidden yourselves as far in the woods as you could. Great Heavens! You might very well all die without a soul coming to help you."

After warming himself for a little while at the stove he approached the bedside. "Well, good mother, so we have taken the notion to be sick, just like people who have money to spend on such things!"

But after a brief examination he ceased to jest, saying:—"She really *is* sick, I do believe."

It was with no affectation that he spoke in the fashion of the peasantry; his grandfather and his father were tillers of the soil, and he had gone straight from the farm to study medicine in Quebec, amongst other young fellows for the most part like himself—grandsons, if not sons of farmers—who had all clung to the plain country manners and the deliberate speech of their fathers. He was tall and heavily built, with a grizzled moustache, and his large face wore the slightly aggrieved expression of one whose native cheerfulness is being continually dashed through listening to the tale of others' ills for which he is bound to show a decent sympathy.

Chapdelaine came in when he had unharnessed and fed the horse. He and his children sat at a little distance while the doctor was going through his programme.

Every one of them was thinking:—"Presently we shall know what is the matter, and the doctor will give her the right medicines." But when the examination was ended, instead of turning to the bottles in his bag, he seemed uncertain and began to ask interminable questions. How had it happened, and where, particularly, did she feel pain . . . Had she ever before suffered from the same trouble . . . The answers did not seem to enlighten him very much; then he turned to the sick woman herself, only to receive confused statements and complaints.

"If it is just a wrench that she has given herself," at length he announced, "she will get well without any meddling; there is nothing for her to do but to stay quietly in bed. But if there is some injury within, to the kidneys or another organ, it may be a grave affair." He was conscious that his state of

[239]

doubt was disappointing to the Chapdelaines,
and was anxious to restore his medical repu-
tation.

"Internal lesions are serious things, and
often one cannot detect them. The wisest
man in the world could tell you no more than
I. We shall have to wait . . . But perhaps
it is not that we have to deal with." After
some further investigation he shook his
head. "Of course I can give something that
will keep her from suffering like this."

The leather bag now disclosed its wonder-
working phials; fifteen drops of a yellowish
drug were diluted with two fingers of water,
and the sick woman, lifted up in bed, managed to swallow this with sharp cries of pain.
Then there was apparently nothing more to
be done; the men lit their pipes, and the
doctor, with his feet against the stove, held
forth as to his professional labours and the
cures he had wrought.

"Illnesses like these," said he, "where one
cannot discover precisely what is the matter,
are more baffling to a doctor than the gravest
disorders—like pneumonia now, or even
typhoid fever which carry off three-quarters

of the people hereabouts who do not die of old age. Well, typhoid and pneumonia, I cure these every month in the year. You know Viateur Tremblay, the postmaster at St. Henri . . ."

He seemed a little hurt that Madame Chapdelaine should be the victim of an obscure malady, hard to diagnose, and had not been taken down with one of the two complaints he was accustomed to treat with such success, and he gave an account by chapter and verse of the manner in which he had cured the postmaster of St. Henri. From that they passed on to the country news—news carried by word of mouth from house to house around Lake St. John, and greeted a thousandfold more eagerly than tidings of wars and famines, since the gossipers always manage to connect it with friend or relative in a country where all ties of kinship, near or far, are borne scrupulously in mind.

Madame Chapdelaine ceased moaning and seemed to be asleep. The doctor, considering that he had done all that was expected of him, for the evening at least, knocked the ashes out of his pipe and rose to go.

"I shall sleep at Honfleur," said he, "I suppose your horse is fit to take me so far? There is no need for you to come, I know the road. I shall stay with Ephrem Surprenant, and come back in the morning."

Chapdelaine was a little slow to make reply, recalling the stiff day's work his old beast had already accomplished, but at the end he went out to harness Charles Eugene once more. In a few minutes the doctor was on the road, leaving the family to themselves as usual.

A great stillness reigned in the house. The comfortable thought was with them all:— "Anyway the medicine he has given her is a good one; she groans no longer." But scarce an hour had gone by before the sick woman ceased to feel the effect of the too feeble drug, became conscious again, tried to turn herself in bed and screamed out with pain. They were all up at once and crowding about her in their concern; she opened her eyes, and after groaning in an agonized way began to weep unrestrainedly.

"O Samuel, I am dying, there can be no doubt of it."

"No! No! You must not think that."

"Yes, I know that I am dying. I feel it. The doctor is only an old fool, and he cannot tell what to do. He is not even able to say what the trouble is, and the medicine he gave me is useless; it has done me no good. I tell you I am dying."

The failing words were hindered with her groaning, and tears coursed down the heavy cheeks. Husband and children looked at her, struck to the very earth with grief. The footstep of death was sounding in the house. They knew themselves cut off from all the world, helpless, remote, without even a horse to bring them succour. The cruel treachery of it all held them speechless and transfixed, with streaming eyes.

In their midst appeared Eutrope Gagnon.

"And I who was thinking to find her almost well. This doctor, now . . ."

Chapdelaine broke out, quite beside himself:—"This doctor is not a bit of use, and I shall tell him so plainly, myself. He came here, he gave her a drop of some miserable stuff worth nothing at all in the bottom of a cup, and he is off to sleep in the village as if his pay was earned! Not a thing has he done but tire out my horse, but he shall not have a copper from me, not a single copper . . ."

Eutrope's face was very grave, and he shook his head as he declared:—"Neither have I any faith in doctors. Now if we had only thought of fetching a bone-setter—such a man as Tit'Sèbe of St. Felicien . . ." Every face was turned to him and the tears ceased flowing.

"Tit'Sèbe!" exclaimed Maria. "And you think he could help in a case like this?" Both Eutrope and Chapdelaine hastened to avow their trust in him.

"There is no doubt whatever that Tit'Sèbe can make people well. He was never through the schools, but he knows how to cure. You heard of Nazaire Gaudreau who fell from the top of a barn and broke his back. The doctors came to see him, and the best they could do was to give the Latin name for his hurt and say that he was going to die. Then they went and fetched Tit'Sèbe, and Tit'Sèbe cured him." Every one of them knew the healer's repute and hope sprang up again in their hearts.

"Tit'Sèbe is a first-rate man, and a man who knows how to make sick people well. Moreover he is not greedy for money. You go and you fetch him, you pay him for his time, and he cures you. It was he who put little Romeo Boilly on his legs again after being run over by a wagon loaded with planks."

The sick woman had relapsed into stupor, and was moaning feebly with her eyes closed.

"I will go and get him if you like," suggested Eutrope.

"But what will you do for a horse?" asked Maria. "The doctor has Charles Eugene at Honfleur."

Chapdelaine clenched his fist in wrath and swore through his teeth:—"The old rascal!"

Eutrope thought a moment before speaking. "It makes no difference. I will go just the same. If I walk to Honfleur, I shall easily find someone there who will lend me a horse and sleigh—Racicot, or perhaps old Neron."

"It is thirty-five miles from here to St. Felicien and the roads are heavy."

"I will go just the same."

He departed forthwith, thinking as he went at a jog-trot over the snow of the grateful look that Maria had given him. The family made ready for the night, computing meanwhile these new distances . . . Seventy miles there and back . . . Roads deep in snow. The lamp was left burning, and till morning the voice from the bed was never hushed. Sometimes it was sharp with pain; sometimes it weakly strove for breath. Two hours after daylight the doctor and the *curé* of St. Henri appeared together.

"It was impossible for me to come sooner," the *curé* explained, "but I am here at last, and I picked up the doctor in the village." They sat at the bedside and talked in low tones. The doctor made a fresh examination, but it was the *curé* who told the result of it. "There is little one can say. She does not seem any worse, but this is not an ordinary sickness. It is best that I should confess her and give her absolution; then we shall both go away and be back again the day after to-morrow."

He returned to the bed, and the others went over and sat by the window. For some minutes the two voices were heard in question

and response; the one feeble and broken by
suffering; the other confident, grave, scarcely
lowered for the solemn interrogation. After
some inaudible words a hand was raised in a
gesture which instantly bowed the heads of
all those in the house. The priest rose.

Before departing the doctor gave Maria a
little bottle with his instructions. "Only if
she should suffer greatly, so that she cries out,
and never more than fifteen drops at a time.
And do not let her have any cold water to
drink."

She saw them to the door, the bottle in her
hand. Before getting into the sleigh the *curé*
took Maria aside and spoke a few words to
her. "Doctors do what they can," said he in
a simple unaffected way, "but only God
Himself has knowledge of disease. Pray with
all your heart, and I shall say a mass for her
to-morrow—a high mass with music, you
understand."

All day long Maria strove to stay the hidden advances of the disorder with her prayers,
and every time that she returned to the bedside it was with a half hope that a miracle had
been wrought, that the sick woman would

cease from her groaning, sleep for a few hours
and awake restored to health. It was not so
to be; the moaning ceased not, but toward
evening it died away to sighing, continual
and profound—nature's protest against a burden too heavy to be borne, or the slow inroad
of death-dealing poison.

About midnight came Eutrope Gagnon,
bringing Tit'Sèbe the bone-setter. He was a
little, thin, sad-faced man with very kind
eyes. As always when called to a sick-bed, he
wore his clothes of ceremony, of dark well-
worn cloth, which he bore with the awkwardness of the peasant in Sunday attire. But the
strong brown hands beyond the thread-bare
sleeves moved in a way to inspire confidence.
They passed over the limbs and body of
Madame Chapdelaine with the most delicate
care, nor did they draw from her a single cry
of pain; thereafter he sat for a long time motionless beside the couch, looking at her as
though awaiting guidance from a source beyond himself. But when at last he broke the
silence it was to say: "Have you sent for the
curé? . . . He has been here. And will he
return? To-morrow; that is well."

After another pause he made his frank avowal:—"There is nothing I can do for her. Something has gone wrong within, about which I know nothing; were there broken bones I could have healed them. I should only have had to feel them with my hands, and then the good God would have told me what to do and I should have cured her. But in this sickness of hers I have no skill. I might indeed put a blister on her back, and perhaps that would draw away the blood and relieve her for a time. Or I could give her a draught made from beaver kidneys; it is useful when the kidneys are affected, as is well known. But I think that neither the blister nor the draught would work a cure."

His speech was so honest and straightforward that he made them one and all feel what manner of thing was a disorder of the human frame—the strangeness and the terror of what is passing behind the closed door, which those without can only fight clumsily as they grope in dark uncertainty.

"She will die if that be God's pleasure."

Maria broke into quiet tears; her father, not yet understanding, sat with his mouth half-open, and neither moved nor spoke. The bone-setter, this sentence given, bowed his head and held his pitiful eyes for long upon the sick woman. The browned hands that now availed him not lay upon his knees; leaning forward a little, his back bent, the gentle sad spirit seemed in silent communion with its maker:—"Thou hast bestowed upon me the gift of healing bones that are broken, and I have healed them; but Thou hast denied me power over such ills as these; so must I let this poor woman die."

For the first time now the deep marks of illness upon the mother's face appeared to husband and children as more than the passing traces of suffering, as imprints from the hand of death. The hard-drawn breath rattling in her throat no longer betokened conscious pain, but was the last blind remonstrance of the body rent by nearing dissolution.

"You do not think she will die before the curé comes back?" Maria asked.

Tit'Sèbe's head and hand showed that he was helpless to answer. "I cannot tell . . . If your horse is able you would do well to seek him with the daylight."

Their eyes searched the window, as yet only a square of darkness, and then returned to her who lay upon the bed . . . But five days ago a hearty, high-spirited woman, in full health of mind and body . . . It could not be that she was to die so soon as that. . . . But knowing now the sad inevitableness, every glance found a subtle change, some fresh token that this bed-ridden woman groaning in her blindness was no more the wife and mother they had known so long.

Half an hour went by; after casting his eyes toward the window Chapdelaine arose hurriedly, saying:—"I am going to put the horse in."

Tit'Sèbe nodded. "That is well; you had better harness; it is near day."

"Yes. I am going to put the horse in," Chapdelaine repeated. But at the moment of his departure it swept over him suddenly that in going to bring the Blessed Sacrament he would be upon a solemn and a final errand, significant of death. The thought held him still irresolute. "I am going to put the horse in." Shifting from foot to foot, he gave a last look at his wife and at length went out.

Not long after the coming of day the wind rose, and soon was sounding hoarsely about the house. "It is from the nor'west; there will be a blow," said Tit'Sèbe.

Maria looked toward the window and sighed. "Only two days ago snow fell, and now it will be raised and drift. The roads were heavy enough before; father and the *curé* are going to have trouble getting through."

But the bone-setter shook his head. "They may have a little difficulty on the road, but they will get here all the same. A priest who brings the Blessed Sacrament has more than the strength of a man." His mild eyes shone with the faith that knows no bounds.

"Yes, power beyond the strength of a man has a priest bearing the Blessed Sacrament. It was three years ago that they summoned me to care for a sick man on the lower Mistassini; at once I saw that I could do nothing for him, and I bade them go fetch a priest. It was night-time and there was not a man in the house, the father himself being sick and his boys quite young. And so at the last it was I that went. On the way back we had to cross the river; the ice had just gone out—it was in

[252]

the spring—and as yet not a boat had been put into the water. We found a great heavy tub that had been lying in the sand all winter, and when we tried to run her down to the water she was buried so deep in the sand and was so heavy that the four of us could not so much as make her budge. Simon Martel was there, big Lalancette of St. Methode, a third I cannot call to mind, and myself; and we four, hauling and shoving to break our hearts as we thought of this poor fellow on the other side of the river who was in the way of dying like a heathen, could not stir that boat a single inch. Well, the *curé* came forward; he laid his hand on the gunwale—just laid his hand on the gunwale, like that—'Give one more shove,' said he; and the boat seemed to start of herself and slipped down to the water as though she were alive. The sick man received the sacrament all right, and died like a Christian just as day was breaking. Yes, a priest has strength beyond the strength of men."

Maria was still sighing, but her heart discovered a melancholy peace in the certainty and nearness of death. This unknown disorder, the dread of what might be coming, these were dark and terrifying phantoms against which one strove blindly, uncomprehendingly. But when one was face to face with death itself all to be done was plain—ordained these many centuries by laws beyond dispute. By day or night, from far or near, the *curé* comes bearing the Holy Sacrament—across angry rivers in the spring, over the treacherous ice, along roads choked with snow, fighting the bitter north-west wind; aided by miracles, he never fails; he fulfils his sacred office, and thenceforward there is room for neither doubt nor fear. Death is but a glorious preferment, a door that opens to the joys unspeakable of the elect.

The wind had risen and was shaking the partitions as window-panes rattle in a sudden gust. The nor'wester came howling over the dark tree-tops, fell upon the clearing about the little wooden buildings—house, stable, barn—in squalls and wicked whirlwinds that sought to lift the roof and smote the walls like a battering-ram, before sweeping onward to the forest in a baffled fury.

The house trembled from base to chimney-
top, and swayed on its foundation in such
a fashion that the inmates, feeling the on-
slaught, hearing the roar and shriek of the foe,
were almost as sensible of the terrors of the
storm as though they were exposed to it;
lacking the consciousness of safe retreat that
belongs to those who are sheltered by strong
walls of stone.

Tit'Sèbe cast his eyes about. "A good
house you have here; tightly made and warm.
Your father and the boys built it, did they
not? Moreover, you must have a good bit of
land cleared by this time . . ."

So loud was the wind that they did not
hear the sound of sleigh-bells, and suddenly
the door flew open against the wall and the
curé of St. Henri entered, bearing the Host
in his raised hands. Maria and Tit'Sébe fell
upon their knees; Tit'Be ran to shut the
door, then also knelt. The priest put off the
heavy fur coat and the cap white with snow
drawn down to his eyes, and instantly approached the sick-bed as heaven's envoy
bringing pardon and peace.

Ah! the assurance, the comfort of the divine promise which dispels the awful mists of death! While the priest performed the sacred rites, and his low words mingled with the sighs of the dying woman, Samuel Chapdelaine and his children were praying with bended heads; in some sort consoled, released from anxiousness and doubt, confident that a sure pact was then concluding with the Almighty for the blue skies of Paradise spangled with stars of gold as a rightful heritage.

Afterwards the *curé* warmed himself by the stove; then they prayed together for a time, kneeling by the bed.

Toward four o'clock the wind leaped to the south-east, and the storm ended swiftly as a broken wave sinks backward from the shore; in the strange deep silence after the tumult the mother sighed, sighed once again, and died.

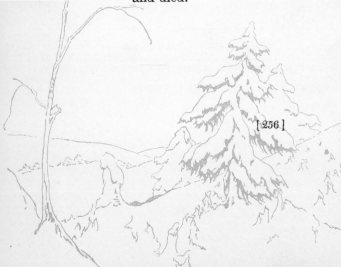

[256]

CHAPTER XV

THAT WE PERISH NOT

CHAPTER XV

THAT WE PERISH NOT

EPHREM SURPRENANT pushed open the door and stood upon the threshold.

"I have come . . ." He found no other words, and waited there motionless for a few seconds, tongue-tied, while his eyes travelled from Chapdelaine to Maria, from Maria to the children who sat very still and quiet by the table; then he plucked off his cap hastily, as if in amends for his forgetfulness, shut the door behind him and moved across to the bed where the dead woman lay.

They had altered its place, turning the head to the wall and the foot toward the centre of the house, so that it might be approached on both sides. Close to the wall two lighted candles stood on chairs; one of them set in a large candlestick of white metal which the visitors to the Chapdelaine home had never seen before, while for holding the other Maria had found nothing better than a

[259]

glass bowl used in the summer time for blueberries and wild raspberries, on days of
ceremony.

The candlestick shone, the bowl sparkled in
the flames which lighted but feebly the face of
the dead. The days of suffering through
which she had passed, or death's final chill
had given the features a strange pallor and
delicacy, the refinement of a woman bred in
the city. Father and children were at first
amazed, and then perceived in this the tremendous consequence of her translation beyond and far above them.

Ephrem Surprenant bent his eyes upon the
face for a little, and then kneeled. The prayers he began to murmur were inaudible, but
when Maria and Tit'Bé came and knelt beside him he drew from a pocket his string of
large beads and began to tell them in a low
voice. The chaplet ended, he sat himself in
silence by the table, shaking his head sadly
from time to time as is seemly in the house of
mourning, and because his own grief was deep
and sincere.

At last he discovered speech. "It is a heavy
loss. You were fortunate in your wife, Sam-

uel; no one may question that. Truly you
were fortunate in your wife."

This said, he could go no further; he sought
in vain for some words of sympathy, and at
the end stumbled into other talk. "The
weather is quite mild this evening; we soon
shall have rain. Everyone is saying that it is
to be an early spring."

To the countryman, all things touching the
soil which gives him bread, and the alternate
seasons which lull the earth to sleep and
awaken it to life, are of such moment that one
may speak of them even in the presence of
death with no disrespect. Their eyes turned
quite naturally to the square of the little
window, but the night was black and they
could discern nothing.

Ephrem Surprenant began anew to praise
her who was departed. "In all the parish
there was not a braver-spirited woman than
she, nor a cleverer housewife. How friendly
too, and what a kind welcome she always gave
a visitor! In the old parishes—yes! and even
in the towns on the railway, not many would
be found to match her. It is only the truth
to say that you were rarely suited in your

wife . . . " Soon afterwards he rose, and, leaving the house, his face was dark with sorrow.

A long silence followed, in which Samuel Chapdelaine's head nodded slowly towards his breast and it seemed as though he were falling asleep. Maria spoke quickly to him, in fear of his offending:—"Father! Do not sleep!"

"No! No!" He sat up straight on his chair and squared his shoulders but since his eyes were closing in spite of him, he stood up hastily, saying:—"Let us recite another chaplet."

Kneeling together beside the bed, they told the chaplet bead by bead. Rising from their knees they heard the rain patter against the window and on the shingles. It was the first spring rain and proclaimed their freedom: the winter ended, the soil soon to reappear, rivers once more running their joyous course, the earth again transformed like some lovely girl released at last from an evil spell by touch of magic wand. But they did not allow themselves to be glad in this house of death, nor indeed did they feel the happiness of it in the midst of their hearts' deep affliction.

Opening the window they moved back to it
and hearkened to the tapping of the great
drops upon the roof. Maria saw that her
father's head had fallen, and that he was very
still; she thought his evening drowsiness was
mastering him again, but when about to
waken him with a word, he it was who sighed
and began to speak.

"Ephrem Surprenant said no more than
the truth. Your mother was a good woman,
Maria; you will not find her like."

Maria's head answered him "Yes," but her
lips were pressed close.

"Full of courage and good counsel, that she
has been throughout her life; but it was
chiefly in the early days after we were married, and then again when Esdras and yourself were little, that she showed herself the
woman she was. The wife of a small farmer
looks for no easy life, but women who take
to their work as well and as cheerfully as she
did in those days, Maria, are hard to
find."

Maria faltered:—"I know, father; I know
it well;" and she dried her eyes for her heart
was melting into tears.

"When we took up our first land at Normandin we had two cows and very little pasture for them, as nearly all our lot was in standing timber and hard to win for the plough. As for me, I picked up my ax and I said to her:—'Laura, I am going to clear land for you.' And from morning till night it was chop, chop, chop, without ever coming back to the house except for dinner; and all that time she did the work of the house and the cooking, she looked after the cattle, mended the fences, cleaned the cow-shed, never rested from her toiling; and then half-a-dozen times a day she would come outside the door and stand for a minute looking at me, over there by the fringe of the woods, where I was putting my back into felling the birches and the spruce to make a patch of soil for her.

"Then in the month of July our well must needs dry up; the cows had not a drop of water to slake their thirst and they almost stopped giving milk. So when I was hard at it in the woods the mother went off to the river with a pail in either hand, and climbed the steep bluff eight or ten times together with these brimming, and her feet that slipped

back in the running sand, till she had filled
a barrel; and when the barrel was full she
got it on a wheelbarrow, and wheeled it off
herself to empty it into the big tub in the
cow-pasture more than three hundred yards
from the house, just below the rocks. It was
not a woman's work, and I told her often
enough to leave it to me, but she always spoke
up briskly:—'Don't you think about that—
don't think about anything—clear a farm for
me.' And she would laugh to cheer me up,
but I saw well enough this was too much for
her, and that she was all dark under the eyes
with the labour of it.

"Well, I caught up my ax and was off to
the woods; and I laid into the birches so
lustily that chips flew as thick as your wrist,
all the time saying to myself that the wife I
had was like no other, and that if the good
God only kept me in health I would make her
the best farm in the countryside."

The rain was ever sounding on the roof;
now and then a gust drove against the window great drops which ran down the panes
like slow-falling tears. Yet a few hours of
rain and the soil would be bare, streams would

dance down every slope; a few more days and they would hear the thundering of the falls.

"When we took up other land above Mistassini," Samuel Chapdelaine continued, "it was the same thing over again; heavy work and hardship for both of us alike; but she was always full of courage and in good heart . . . We were in the midst of the forest, but as there were some open spaces of rich grass among the rocks we took to raising sheep. One evening . . ." He was silent for a little, and when he began speaking again his eyes were fixed intently upon Maria, as though he wished to make very clear to her what he was about to say.

"It was in September; the time when all the great creatures of the woods become dangerous. A man from Mistassini who was coming down the river in a canoe landed near our place and spoke to us thiswise:—'Look after your sheep; the bears came and killed a heifer last week quite close to the houses.' So your mother and I went off that evening to the pasture to drive the sheep into the pen for the night so that the bears would not devour them.

"I took one side and she the other, as the
sheep used to scatter among the alders.   It
was growing dark, and suddenly I heard
Laura cry out: 'Oh, the scoundrels!' Some
animals were moving in the bushes, and it was
plain to see they were not sheep. because in
the woods toward evening sheep are white
patches. So, ax in hand, I started off running
as hard as I could. Later on, when we were on
the way back to the house, your mother told
me all about it. She had come across a sheep
lying dead, and two bears that were just going to eat it. Now it takes a pretty good man,
one not easily frightened and with a gun in his
hand, to face a bear in September; as for a
woman empty-handed, the best thing she can
do is to run for it and not a soul will blame
her. But your mother snatched a stick from
the ground and made straight for the bears,
screaming   at   them:—'Our   beautiful   fat
sheep! Be off with you, you ugly thieves, or
I will do for you!' I got there at my best
speed, leaping over the stumps; but by that
time the bears had cleared off into the woods
without showing fight, scared as could be, because she had put the fear of death into them."

Maria listened breathlessly; asking herself if it was really her mother who had done this thing—the mother whom she had always known so gentle and tender-hearted; who had never given Telesphore a little rap on the head without afterwards taking him on her knees to comfort him, adding her own tears to his, and declaring that to slap a child was something to break one's heart.

The brief spring shower was already spent; through the clouds the moon was showing her face—eager to discover what was left of the winter's snow after this earliest rain. As yet the ground was everywhere white; the night's deep silence told them that many days must pass before they would hear again the dull roaring of the cataract; but the tempered breeze whispered of consolation and promise.

Samuel Chapdelaine lapsed into silence for a while, his head bowed, his hands resting upon his knees, dreaming of the past with its toilsome years that were yet so full of brave hopes. When he took up his tale it was in a voice that halted, melancholy with self-reproach.

"At Normandin, at Mistassini and the other places we have lived I always worked hard; no one can say nay to that. Many an acre of forest have I cleared and I have built houses and barns, always saying to myself that one day we should have a comfortable farm where your mother would live as do the women in the old parishes, with fine smooth fields all about the house as far as the eye could see, a kitchen garden, handsome well-fed cattle in the farm-yard . . . And, after it all, here is she dead in this half-savage spot, leagues from other houses and churches, and so near the bush that some nights one can hear the foxes bark. And it is my fault that she has died so . . . My fault . . . My fault." Remorse seized him; he shook his head at the pity of it, his eyes upon the floor.

"Many times it happened, after we had spent five or six years in one place and all had gone well, that we were beginning to get together a nice property—good pasturage, broad fields ready for sowing, a house lined inside with pictures from the papers . . . Then people came and settled about us; we had but to wait a little, working on quietly,

[269]

and soon we should have been in the midst of
a well-to-do settlement where Laura could
have passed the rest of her days in happiness
. . . And then all of a sudden I lost heart; I
grew sick and tired of my work and of the
countryside; I began to hate the very faces
of those who had taken up land near-by and
used to come to see us, thinking that we
should be pleased to have a visitor after being
so long out of the way of them. I heard people saying that farther off toward the head
of the Lake there was good land in the forest;
that some folk from St. Gedeon spoke of settling over on that side; and forthwith I began
to hunger and thirst for this spot they were
talking about, that I had never seen in my life
and where not a soul lived, as for the place of
my birth . . .

"Well, in those days, when the work was
done, instead of smoking beside the stove I
would go out to the door-step and sit there
without moving, like a man homesick and
lonely; and everything I saw in front of me—
the place I had made with these two hands
after so much of labour and sweat—the fields,
the fences, over to the rocky knoll that shut

us in—I detested them all till I seemed ready to go out of my mind at the very sight of them.

"And then your mother would come quietly up behind me. She also would look out across our place, and I knew that she was pleased with it to the bottom of her heart because it was beginning to look like the old parish where she had grown up, and where she would so gladly have spent her days. But instead of telling me that I was no better than a silly old fool for wishing to leave—as most women would have done—and finding hard things to say about my folly, she only sighed a little as she thought of the drudgery that was to begin all over again somewhere back in the woods, and kindly and softly she would say to me:—'Well, Samuel! Are we soon to be on the move once more?' When she said that I could not answer, for I was speechless with very shame at thinking of the wretched life I had given her; but I knew well enough that it would end in our moving again and pushing on to the north, deeper into the woods, and that she would be with me and take her share in this hard business of beginning anew—

[271]

as cheerful and capable and good-humoured as ever, without one single word of reproach or spitefulness."

He was silent after that, and seemed to ponder long his sorrow and the things which might have been. Maria, sighing, passed a hand across her face as though she would brush away a disquieting vision; but in very truth there was nothing she wished to forget. What she heard had moved her profoundly, and she felt in a dim and troubled way that this story of a hard life so bravely lived had for her a deep and timely significance and held some lesson if only she might understand it.

"How little do we know people!" was the thought that filled her mind. Since her mother had crossed the threshold of death she seemed to wear a new aspect, not of this world; and now all the homely and familiar traits endearing her to them were being over-shadowed by other virtues well-nigh heroic in their quality.

To pass her days in these lonely places when she would have dearly loved the society of other human beings and the unbroken peace of village life; to strive from dawn till

nightfall, spending all her strength in a
thousand heavy tasks, and yet from dawn till
nightfall never losing patience nor her happy
tranquillity; continually to see about her
only the wilderness, the great pitiless forest,
and to hold in the midst of it all an ordered
way of life, the gentleness and the joyousness
which are the fruits of many a century sheltered from such rudeness—was it not surely
a hard thing and a worthy? And the recom-
pense? After death, a little word of
praise.

Was it worth the cost? The question
scarcely framed itself with such clearness in
her mind, but so her thoughts were tending.
Thus to live, as hardly, as courageously, and
to be so sorely missed when she departed, few
women were fit for this. As for herself . . .

The sky, flooded with moonlight, was of a
wonderful lambency and depth; across the
whole arch of heaven a band of cloud, fash-
ioned strangely into carven shapes, defiled
in solemn march. The white ground no longer
spoke of chill and desolateness, for the air was
soft; and by some magic of the approaching
spring the snow appeared to be only a mask

covering the earth's face, in nowise terrifying
—a mask one knew must soon be lifted.

Maria seated by the little window fixed her
unconscious eyes upon the sky and the fields
stretching away whitely to the environing
woods, and of a sudden it was borne to her
that the question she was asking herself had
just received its answer. To dwell in this land
as her mother had dwelt, and, dying thus, to
leave behind her a sorrowing husband and a
record of the virtues of her race, she knew in
her heart she was fit for that. In reckoning
with herself there was no trace of vanity;
rather did the response seem from without.
Yes, she was able; and she was filled with
wonderment as though at the shining of
some unlooked-for light.

Thus she too could live; but . . . it was
not as yet in her heart so to do . . . In a
little while, this season of mourning at an end,
Lorenzo Surprenant would come back from
the States for the third time and would bear
her away to the unknown delights of the city
—away from the great forest she hated—
away from that cruel land where men who go
astray perish helplessly, where women endure

endless torment the while ineffectual aid is sought for them over the long roads buried in snow. Why should she stay here to toil and suffer when she might escape to the lands of the south and a happier life?

The soft breeze telling of spring came against the window, bringing a confusion of gentle sounds; the swish and sigh of branches swaying and touching one another, the distant hooting of an owl. Then the great silence reigned once more. Samuel Chapdelaine was sleeping; but in this repose beside the dead was nothing unseemly or wanting in respect; chin fallen on his breast, hands lying open on his knees, he seemed to be plunged into the very depths of sorrow or striving to relinquish life that he might follow the departed a little way into the shades.

Again Maria asked herself:—"Why stay here, to toil and suffer thus? Why? . . ." And when she found no answer, it befell at length that out of the silence and the night voices arose.

No miraculous voices were these; each of us hears them when he goes apart and withdraws himself far enough to escape from the petty turmoil of his daily life. But they speak more loudly and with plainer accents to the simple-hearted, to those who dwell among the great northern woods and in the empty places of the earth. While yet Maria was dreaming of the city's distant wonders the first voice brought murmuringly to her memory a hundred forgotten charms of the land she wished to flee.

The marvel of the reappearing earth in the springtime after the long months of winter . . . The dreaded snow stealing away in prankish rivulets down every slope; the tree-roots first resurgent, then the mosses drenched with wet, soon the ground freed from its burden whereon one treads with delighted glances and sighs of happiness like the sick man who feels glad life returning to his veins . . . Later yet, the birches, alders, aspens swelling into bud; the laurel clothing itself in rosy bloom . . . The rough battle with the soil a seeming holiday to men no longer condemned to idleness; to draw the hard breath of toil from morn till eve a gracious favour . . .

—The cattle, at last set free from their shed, gallop to the pasture and glut themselves with the fresh grass. All the new-born creatures—the calves, the fowls, the lambs, gambol in the sun and add daily to their stature like the hay and the barley. The poorest farmer sometimes halts in yard or field, hands in pockets, and tastes the great happiness of knowing that the sun's heat, the warm rain, the earth's unstinted alchemy —every mighty force of nature—is working as a humble slave for him . . . for him.

—And then, the summertide; the glory of sunny noons, the heated quivering air that blurs the horizon and the outline of the forest, the flies swarming and circling in the sun's rays, and but three hundred paces from the house the rapids and the fall—white foam against dark water—the mere sight of it filling one with a delicious coolness. In its due time the harvest; the grain that gives life heaped into the barns; then autumn and soon the returning winter . . . But here was the marvel of it, that the winter seemed no longer abhorrent or terrifying; it brought in its train the sweet intimacies of a house shut fast, and beyond the door, with the sameness and the

soundlessness of deep-drifted snow, peace, a
great peace . . .

In the cities were the strange and wonderful things whereof Lorenzo Surprenant had
told, with others that she pictured to herself
confusedly: wide streets suffused with light,
gorgeous shops, an easy life of little toil with a
round of small pleasures and distractions.
Perhaps, though, one would come to tire of
this restlessness, and, yearning some evening
only for repose and quiet, where would one
discover the tranquillity of field and wood, the
soft touch of that cooler air that draws from
the north-west after set of sun, the wide-
spreading peacefulness that settles on the
earth sinking to untroubled sleep.

"And yet they must be beautiful!" thought
she, still dreaming of those vast American
cities . . . As though in answer, a second
voice was raised.

—Over there was it not a stranger land
where people of an alien race spoke of unfamiliar things in another tongue, sang other
songs? Here . . .

—The very names of this her country, those
she listened to every day, those heard but

[278]

once, came crowding to memory: a thousand names piously bestowed by peasants from France on lakes, on rivers, on the settlements of the new country they were discovering and peopling as they went—lac à l'Eau-Claire—la Famine — Saint-Cœur-de-Marie — Trois-Pistoles—Sainte Rose-du-Dégel—Pointe-aux-Outardes—Saint-André-de-l'Epouvante . . . An uncle of Eutrope Gagnon's lived at Saint-André-de-l'Epouvante; Racicot of Honfleur spoke often of his son who was a stoker on a Gulf coaster, and every time new names were added to the old; names of fishing villages and little harbours on the St. Lawrence, scattered here and there along those shores between which the ships of the old days had boldly sailed toward an unknown land—Pointe-Mille-Vaches—les Escoumins—Notre-Dame-du-Portage—les Grandes-Bergeronnes—Gaspé.

—How sweet to hear these names where one was talking of distant acquaintance and kinsfolk, or telling of far journeys! How dear and neighbourly was the sound of them, with a heart-warming friendly ring that made one feel as he spoke them:—"Throughout all this land we are at home . . . at home . . ."

—Westward, beyond the borders of the Province; southward, across the line were everywhere none but English names. In time one might learn to speak them, even might they at last come familiarly to the ear; but where should one find again the happy music of the French names?

—Words of a foreign speech from every lip, on every street, in every shop . . . Little girls taking hands to dance a round and singing a song one could not understand . . . Here . . .

Maria turned toward her father who still slept with his chin sunk on his breast, looking like a man stricken down by grief whose meditation is of death; and the look brought her swift memory of the hymns and country songs he was wont to teach his children in the evenings.

> A la claire fontaine
> M'en allant promener . . .

In those cities of the States, even if one taught the children how to sing them would they not straightway forget!

The clouds a little while ago drifting singly across a moonlit sky were now spread over the

heavens in a vast filmy curtain, and the dim
light passing through it was caught by the
earth's pale coverlet of melting snow; between
the two wan expanses the ranks of the forest
darkly stretched their long battle-front.

Maria shuddered; the emotion which had
glowed in her heart was dying; once again she
said to herself: "And yet it is a harsh land, this
land of ours . . . Why should I linger here?"

Then it was that a third voice, mightier
than the others, lifted itself up in the silence:
the voice of Quebec—now the song of a
woman, now the exhortation of a priest. It
came to her with the sound of a church bell,
with the majesty of an organ's tones, like a
plaintive love-song, like the long high call of
woodsmen in the forest. For verily there was
in it all that makes the soul of the Province:
the loved solemnities of the ancestral faith;
the lilt of that old speech guarded with jealous
care; the grandeur and the barbaric strength
of this new land where an ancient race has
again found its youth.

Thus spake the voice:—"Three hundred
years ago we came, and we have remained . . .
They who led us hither might return among

us without knowing shame or sorrow, for if it be true that we have little learned, most surely nothing is forgot.

"We bore oversea our prayers and our songs; they are ever the same. We carried in our bosoms the hearts of the men of our fatherland, brave and merry, easily moved to pity as to laughter, of all human hearts the most human; nor have they changed. We traced the boundaries of a new continent, from Gaspé to Montreal, from St. Jean d'Iberville to Ungava, saying as we did it:—Within these limits all we brought with us, our faith, our tongue, our virtues, our very weaknesses are henceforth hallowed things which no hand may touch, which shall endure to the end.

"Strangers have surrounded us whom it is our pleasure to call foreigners; they have taken into their hands most of the rule, they have gathered to themselves much of the wealth; but in this land of Quebec nothing has changed. Nor shall anything change, for we are the pledge of it. Concerning ourselves and our destiny but one duty have we clearly understood: that we should hold fast—should endure. And we have held fast, so that, it may

[282]

be, many centuries hence the world will look
upon us and say:—These people are of a race
that knows not how to perish . . . We are
a testimony.

"For this is it that we must abide in that
Province where our fathers dwelt, living as
they have lived, so to obey the unwritten
command that once shaped itself in their
hearts, that passed to ours, which we in turn
must hand on to descendants innumerable:—
In this land of Quebec naught shall die and
naught shall suffer change . . ."

The veil of gray cloud which hid the whole
heavens had become heavier and more lour-
ing, and suddenly the rain began afresh,
bringing yet a little nearer that joyous hour
when the earth would lie bare and the rivers
be freed. Samuel Chapdelaine slept profoundly, his head sunk upon his breast, an
old man yielding at last to the long fatigues
of his lifetime of toil. Above the candlestick
of metal and the glass bowl the candle flames
wavered under gentle breaths from the window, and shadows flitting across the face of
the dead woman made her lips seem to be
moving in prayer or softly telling secrets.

[283]

Maria Chapdelaine awaked from her dream to the thought:—"So I shall stay—shall stay here after all!" For the voices had spoken commandingly and she knew she could not choose but obey. It was only then that the recollection of other duties came, after she had submitted, and a sigh had passed her lips. Alma Rose was still a child; her mother dead, there must be a woman in the house. But in truth it was the voices which had told her the way.

The rain was pattering on the roof, and nature, rejoicing that winter was past, sent soft little wandering airs through the casement as though she were sighing in content. Throughout the hours of the night Maria moved not; with hands folded in her lap, patient of spirit and without bitterness, yet dreaming a little wistfully of the far-off wonders her eyes would never behold and of the land wherein she was bidden to live with its store of sorrowful memories; of the living flame which her heart had known awhile and lost forever, and the deep snowy woods whence too daring youths shall no more return.

CHAPTER XVI

PLEDGED TO THE RACE

CHAPTER XVI

PLEDGED TO THE RACE

ESDRAS and Da'Bé came down from the shanties in May, and their grieving brought freshly to the household the pain of bereavement. But the naked earth was lying ready for the seed, and mourning must not delay the season's labours.

Eutrope Gagnon was there one evening to pay them a visit, and a glance he stole at Maria's face perhaps told him of a change in her, for when they were alone he put the question:—"Maria, do you still think of going away?"

Her eyes were lowered, as with a motion of her head she signified "No."

"Then . . . I know well that this is no time to speak of such things, but if only you could say there would be a chance for me one day, then could I bear the waiting better."

And Maria answered him:—"Yes . . .

If you wish I will marry you as you asked me to . . . In the spring—the spring after this spring now—when the men come back from the woods for the sowing."